149

J3

Weekly Reader Cl

D0426211

Snowed Up

WEEKLY READER
CHILDREN'S BOOK CLUB
This is a registered trademark

BY ROSALIE K. FRY

Promise of the Rainbow
Whistler in the Mist
Snowed Up

Rosalie K. Fry

Snowed Up

ILLUSTRATED BY ROBIN JACQUES

Farrar, Straus & Giroux · New York
An Ariel Book

Copyright © 1970 by Rosalie K. Fry

All rights reserved
SBN 374.3.7100.8
Library of Congress catalog card number: 76-125142
Printed in the United States of America
Weekly Reader Children's Book Club Edition

Snowed Up

1

THE first small snowflake wavered uncertainly past the window, followed by a little burst of larger flakes.

"It is . . . it really is beginning to snow at last!" cried Anna, her dark eyes sparkling as she sprang across the room.

But Verity reached the window first, flinging herself across the back of the couch to press her forehead against the ice-cold glass. Even Brian dragged his attention from the fascinating pages of his new Welsh-English dictionary to smile hopefully toward the window, although as usual he was silent. But thirteen-year-old Susan turned with a quick little frown and said flatly: "Well, I hoped it wouldn't snow."

Anna looked at her sister in dismay. Susan was little more than a year older than herself, but she was growing up already—grown-up people never really wanted snow.

Verity was nine and a half, and she had been hoping for days that it would snow. She now whirled around from the window, two bright spots of angry color appearing in her cheeks as she faced Susan.

"Well, you jolly well ought to want it, for Brian's sake," she burst out accusingly. "He's only got three more weeks with us anyway, and once he gets back home to Australia he might never see snow again for the rest of his whole life."

"Oh, I hope not the rest of his life!" laughed Aunt Marian, putting plates in the oven to warm. "Brian's mother grew up on this farm with your mother and me, remember, so he belongs here the same as the rest of you. I certainly hope he'll get back here to Wales again one day."

"Well, even if he does, I bet it won't be for years and years, and by then it will be too late. He'll be even older than Susan, so he probably won't like snow any better than she does."

"I'm sorry, but I still don't want it, even for Brian's sake," said Susan, coming to the table with her hands full of knives and spoons. "Uncle Fred's sheep are a good deal more important than snowballing," she added in her most infuriatingly grown-up manner.

Verity gave her one look, then hunched her shoulders

and turned back to watch the snow, which was whirling down in earnest now and getting thicker every minute.

"Well, if it's coming it'll come, whether we want it or whether we don't," observed Aunt Marian sensibly. "And if it really lies," she went on, glancing at Verity's angry back, "then I'll be able to make something your grandmother used to make for all of us when we were children."

"What?" asked Verity, turning around from the window, her anger forgotten in curiosity.

"Snow pancakes. And that's something Brian could never get in Australia, although I'm sure his mother must remember having them here when she was young."

"I've never heard of snow pancakes. How are they made?" asked Susan.

"Exactly like ordinary pancakes, except that you use snow instead of milk. And I don't know what the snow does to them, but they are the nicest pancakes you ever tasted, and light—I never knew anything quite so light.

"But now I mustn't stand gossiping here. I think I'd best see to your uncle's breakfast first, if the rest of you don't mind waiting. And here he comes," she added, glancing up as her husband appeared in the doorway.

"I'll have to be off up the hill right away and fetch the sheep down in case this comes on heavy," he announced.

"Where are they? Not still up the mountain?"

"Oh no. I brought them down as far as Pen Mynydd last week. But the weather looks really bad this morning.

I'll be happier to have them down here in the field below, where I can keep an eye on them."

"Well, at least have your breakfast before you go. I have it ready here." And Aunt Marian pulled the kettle forward.

"Oh, I guess I'd better not wait," he began, hesitating in the doorway. But she cut him short.

"Now, Fred, don't be ridiculous," she said crisply. "Ten minutes isn't going to make a scrap of difference to the sheep, one way or the other, but a good hot meal is going to make all the difference to you, and that I do know. So come along in, for pity's sake—there's a wicked draft from that door."

She bustled between the stove and the table as she talked, making tea and scooping eggs and bacon onto a dim old willow-pattern plate, which she put down in front of her husband as he lowered himself into his chair.

"And here's your tea. I've sugared it ready," she added, putting the cup beside him.

"Funny you say *down* to Pen Mynydd, when 'pen' means top and 'mynydd' is a mountain," mused Brian, quite unaware that Susan was trying to lay the table around him as he sat sprawled over his dictionary.

"Not so funny, really," replied his uncle, smiling. "It's the same as an English farm might be called Hill Top. It'd be a mountain farm most probably, but even so, it would be some way below the actual summit. A farm needs shelter, remember."

"Now," said Aunt Marian, turning to the children, "I suppose the rest of you will want eggs only, same as usual? Never mind," she added, laughing. "I'll be sending you home with a nice piece of home-cured bacon. Your mother knows what's good, even if you town-bred children don't! And if you want to start with cornflakes, you'll need more milk—perhaps you'll fetch it from the dairy, Brian. It's the blue jug on the stone slab."

As Brian ambled away with his book tucked under his arm, the others pulled up their chairs to the table. Susan fetched cornflakes from the cupboard and handed out the bowls.

"I get 'Remember me,' " said Verity, picking out an old pink bowl with the words in faded gilt lettering around the rim.

"What on earth can Brian be up to?" said Susan presently. "I bet he can't see the jug right in front of his nose. I'll have to fetch it myself." And she whisked away out the door.

"That boy's a sight too clever—always got his head in a book," observed Aunt Marian with a disapproving shake of her head.

"Too clever? I didn't know anyone could be too clever. At school they never seem to think I'm clever enough," sighed Verity.

"You're a grasshopper, that's your trouble," teased her uncle.

Verity considered this for a moment, but before she

could decide on an answer, she was off on another question: "Is Brian even cleverer than Susan?"

"Ah, Susan is a different type entirely," said Aunt Marian with a quick warm smile. "I've never known a thirteen-year-old, boy or girl, as sensible as Susan."

"Must take after her aunt," remarked Uncle Fred, winking at Verity as the two returned from the dairy, Susan carrying the jug.

"Won't you come and have your own breakfast now, Aunt Marian?" urged Susan presently. "Your tea will be getting cold."

"Yes, yes, I'll come directly, dear, but I want to see to your uncle first. Wait, Fred, I'll fetch your crook from the barn while you get your boots on."

"Never knew such a little woman, always thinks of everything," remarked Uncle Fred as his wife's quick footsteps echoed back from the flagstone passage outside. But a moment later they were startled to hear a sudden sharp cry, and running out, they found her lying in the yard.

"Careful! It's a sheet of ice." She just managed to gasp the warning before collapsing with a little moan of pain.

"It's my leg," she whispered, as her husband knelt beside her. "I'm afraid it may be broken. Oh, Fred, whatever can we do, with the sheep to see to, and the children here and all?"

"We'll be perfectly all right. I'll look after the others," promised Susan, dragging off her apron and holding it over her aunt in an attempt to protect her from the driving snow.

"Now, Marian, don't you fret about anything," soothed Uncle Fred. "First of all we must get you in out of the snow. Wait, though," he cautioned, as Brian stepped forward to help. "We mustn't lift her yet, not if any bones are broken."

He studied the awkwardly twisted leg in silence for a moment, then stood up and said quietly: "I reckon we'd best bind this leg very carefully to the good one, and then tie the two to some sort of splint for extra support before we attempt to move her."

"Here, you two!" he called to the scared pair in the doorway. "Will one of you find me a long straight stick to use as a splint? A broom handle will do, anything you can find. Then we'll need something soft to use as binding, a couple of towels, say—"

"Not good towels, mind," interrupted Aunt Marian feebly.

"Well, rags then, anything, just so long as it's softish," he said. "Meanwhile, Brian, if you'll come with me, there's half an old door in the barn. We could use that as a stretcher, I guess."

"And will one of you fetch out some coats to keep off the snow? This apron's useless," Susan called after her sisters as they darted indoors, thankful to have something to do.

When they returned with the coats and broom and a

couple of threadbare towels, Uncle Fred sent them scurrying back to prepare the kitchen for Aunt Marian.

"Push the table back, right out of the way," he directed. "We'll need a good clear space so we can put the stretcher down in front of the fire."

"And you might find a cushion to put under her head," called Susan, "and fill up the kettle so we can give her a hot bottle."

When the kitchen was clear, Anna punched the fat, embroidered cushions on the couch.

"Not soft enough. Better get feather pillows off the beds," she decided, leading the way upstairs.

"And an eiderdown might be nice to keep her extra warm," suggested Verity, gathering the billowing folds into her arms and trailing after Anna as she went downstairs with the pillows and an empty hot-water bottle.

They found Aunt Marian already installed in the kitchen, lying back against a folded coat with her eyes closed. She looked so white and shaken that they crept in on tiptoe and stood about, afraid to speak, while Susan made her comfortable with the pillows. Then she filled the hot-water bottle, testing it critically to make sure it was not too hot.

"There, you warm your cold hands on that," she said gently, placing the bottle carefully against her aunt's side.

Anna watched wistfully, wondering how it was that Susan always knew just what to do and how to do it.

Aunt Marian was already reviving under her care, and presently she opened her eyes and murmured gratefully: "Ah, that's better." Then, with a ghost of her old bright smile, she went on. "And now we must decide what's to be done for the best."

"Well, the first thing to be done is to get you into the hospital," said Uncle Fred. "And it's no use looking at me like that, my girl. Your leg has not only got to be set, but you'll need proper care afterwards. It looks a pretty nasty break to me."

"But the sheep . . ."

"It won't hurt the sheep to wait, as you said yourself. Anyhow, I'll go down to the kiosk and phone for the ambulance right away."

"Ambulance?"

"Certainly. I'm not jolting you all the way down to the hospital in the Land Rover with that leg," he replied, opening the door.

"Mind the ice, then, and put on your coat," she called after him.

Aunt Marian soon discovered that as long as she kept perfectly still, she could organize things from where she lay. Her first suggestion came as a shock to the children.

"I'm sorry to have to say this, my dears, but I'm afraid it will really be best for you to go home today, instead of on Friday as planned."

There was a gasp from Verity, quickly suppressed by a frown from Susan.

"I know. It's dreadfully disappointing for us all," Aunt Marian agreed. "But, you see, Uncle Fred will be out half the day with the sheep, and he'll only fret if he knows you are here with nobody to look after you."

"But Susan is just like a grown-up person, and she and Anna both learned cooking at school," Verity pointed out.

But Aunt Marian was accustomed to making arrangements for everyone, and although she smiled, her mind was made up.

"Yes, but it isn't just the cooking. Poor old Fred is such a worrier, so we've got to make things as easy for him as we can."

Verity opened her mouth as if to speak again, but Susan shot her a warning glance as Aunt Marian went on: "Now the point is, how do those long-distance coaches run?"

"There are two a day," said Susan, "the one at 11 a.m. that we were planning to catch on Friday, and another at three in the afternoon. The eleven o'clock one gets us home just before four."

"Then that's the one you'd better catch. I'd rather you got home in daylight. What time is it now? Nine forty-five? Well, that should give you time. Your mother will be at home today, I suppose?"

"Oh yes, she's always in on a Monday. It's Aunt Myra's day for coming over," answered Susan.

"Good. Then you may as well arrive home unan-

nounced—no need to alarm your mother with a telegram."

"She'd be sure to think someone had died if we sent a
telegram," put in Verity with a sudden grin.

"I know," said Aunt Marian with a smile. "So now
I suggest Susan prepare a picnic lunch for the journey
while you others get your packing done upstairs."

2

*B*Y the time the children reached the landing, slow tears were running down Verity's cheeks.

"Don't cry. I'm sure she's going to be all right," said Anna soothingly.

"I wasn't thinking about Aunt Marian, actually," gulped Verity guiltily. "It's the snow. I want to stay so desperately."

"I know. I do too," said Anna. "But it's no use trying to go against Aunt Marian once she's set on something. I expect Susan's right when she says because Aunt Marian has no children she spends all her energies in looking after Uncle Fred and shielding him from worry."

"I can't see why he'd need to worry if we stayed here to make his bed and fetch in coal and cook for him," muttered Verity obstinately.

"Yes, but she *thinks* he'd worry, that's the point. And now she's hurt it's up to us to make things easy for her," explained Anna patiently.

"But why, oh why need it happen now in the snow?" wailed Verity. "We never get proper snow at home, or if we do the traffic turns it into slush before we have time to enjoy it. And we might never be here in snow again," she sobbed despairingly. "It's nearly always summer when we come."

"It's worse for me—we don't even get slush in my part of Australia," said Brian, turning gloomily into his room.

"Ah well, we'd better get packed, I suppose. Come, Verity," said Anna, leading the way to the bedroom they were sharing. They shared a little suitcase too, and their few belongings were soon packed.

"We'll be wearing all our bulky things, like anoraks and Wellingtons," she said. "And Sue is sure to make us wear our raincoats, too, until we are actually in the coach. Well, that seems to be everything in this room. We'd better go and see how Brian is getting on. I wouldn't be a bit surprised if he's completely forgotten what he came upstairs to do."

They found their cousin standing in the middle of his room with his hands hanging helplessly at his sides.

"Oh, Brian, you haven't even started!" accused Anna, trying not to laugh.

"How can I? Just look at all this." And he waved his

hand despondently toward the chest of drawers, which was covered with the delicate pieces of a half-made model plane.

"Whatever is it?" cried Verity, darting forward.

"Careful—don't touch!" he warned, putting out a hand to ward her off.

"I just can't see how I'm to pack it all," he went on. "I'd never have started assembling the thing, but I thought we'd be here till Friday, which would have given me plenty of time."

"What is it, anyway?" repeated Verity.

"A model biplane. I got the kit in London with my Christmas money."

"And you're making it yourself?" said Anna, much impressed.

"Oh, they're not difficult to make, once you get the hang of the technical terms used in the instructions. But of course the really exciting part is flying the thing when it's made."

"Flying? You mean this model will really fly?" cried Verity.

"Of course. No point in making something that doesn't work."

"How far can it fly?"

"Maybe a mile or so. Hard to judge, as I have to keep it circling around and around on a long string. If I let it fly free, I'd probably never find it again."

"How long does it take to make a whole plane?" asked

Anna, studying the intricate pieces spread out on the chest.

"Oh, not too long. You get better with every one you make, of course. I only started this on Saturday. I've been working on it before breakfast the last three mornings."

"But why up here in the cold?" asked Anna. "Wouldn't it be easier on the table downstairs?"

A slow grin spread over Brian's face. "Somehow I don't think Aunt Marian would really appreciate all this on her kitchen table when she's busy cooking," he replied. "We'd probably find ourselves picking bits of balsa wood out of the mashed potatoes or a tail plane out of the stew!"

Verity giggled, but Brian went on more soberly. "Anyway, how in the world am I going to pack this lot? I only brought it here because I thought this would be such a super place to fly it."

"Mmm, much better than back at our house," agreed Verity. "I can see it crashing into a bus on its very first flight at home."

Anna climbed onto a chair and began pulling the lids off a number of cardboard boxes stacked on top of the wardrobe. "How about this?" she asked, handing down an empty box. "It's even got some tissue paper in it. I'm sure Aunt Marian will let you have it."

"Ah, just the job," said Brian gratefully. "I'd better pack it myself, though," he went on quickly, guessing that Verity was dying for a chance to get her hands on the fragile pieces.

A step sounded on the stairs and Anna remembered the packing.

"I say, we'd better get on," she whispered guiltily, and falling on her knees, she began tossing pajamas and socks into Brian's suitcase, while Verity scooped a jumble of string and mechanics magazines out of a gaping drawer.

"I'd better have that," said Brian, pouncing on the ball of string and stuffing it into his pocket, while Anna reached for the magazines.

Susan put her head around the door. "Ah good, you're getting on," she said approvingly. "Now listen. Aunt Marian and I have been talking things over, and we've decided on a change of plan."

"You mean we're staying?" interrupted Verity, her eyes alight with the sudden hope.

"No, you three are going home as planned. But I am staying, after all. Aunt Marian had so many worries on her mind that she was really relieved when I suggested staying to keep up the fire for Uncle Fred, and cook him something hot when he comes in, and feed the hens, and so on."

"Oh, you lucky dab!" exploded Verity enviously. "But why should you be the one to stay when you're the only one who doesn't like the snow?"

"Don't be silly. Of course it must be Sue," said Anna impatiently. "You know she's the only one who could look after things properly here. I can't cook enough to look after Uncle Fred, and I wouldn't have a clue about the hens' food, or how to manage the kitchen range, or anything."

"Well now, if you're ready, you'd better take your things downstairs and get your Wellingtons," continued Susan, glancing around the room. "Oh, look, Anna, you've left a slipper behind the door—and isn't that a hankie under the bed?"

"I'll follow you down in a minute," she went on. "But I must go along first to Aunt Marian's room and pack up the things she'll need for the hospital." And she hurried away.

"Why can't I ever do things as well as Susan?" muttered Anna, jamming the offending slipper into the suitcase before running downstairs after Verity.

"Got all your things?" asked Aunt Marian as the two came into the kitchen. "I only hope you'll be all right. I must say I'd feel easier in my mind if Susan was going to be there to look after you all."

"But why should we need looking after in a coach full of grown-up people?" asked Verity.

"Yes, it's silly of me, I suppose. But Susan is always so dependable and takes such splendid care of you all that it's hard to picture you managing without her. Anyhow, it will be up to you now, Anna. There'll be no Susan to shelter behind today. You'll be the eldest now, remember."

"Only a few months the eldest," said Anna hastily, alarmed at the prospect of being in charge of anyone.

Aunt Marian shook her head as she replied, "My dear child, can you seriously imagine vague old Brian looking after anybody, whatever his age? He's scarcely able to look after himself, let alone anyone else."

Upstairs, Brian was wrapping his model piece by piece in tissue paper, stowing each with unhurried care in the cardboard box. He then fitted this into the space Anna had left for it in the middle of his suitcase and followed the others down to the kitchen.

"Aunt Marian says you may keep that box," Verity informed him. "And if—" She broke off with a sudden peal of laughter as the far door opened and their uncle stamped into the room, scattering snow as he came.

"Oh, Uncle Fred, you're white all over!" she exclaimed. "Do you know you've even got snow on your eyebrows? It makes you look just like Father Christmas!"

But Uncle Fred was far too cold to care what he looked like.

"Ambulance won't be long," he said briefly, striding across to warm his hands at the fire. Suddenly he caught sight of the three children standing with their luggage and demanded in surprise: "But what's all this then?"

"I've decided it will be best for them to go home today," explained Aunt Marian. "Susan is staying to look after you here, while the other three go home on the eleven o'clock coach."

"Well now, I don't see as there's any need for them to go," he began, but Aunt Marian cut in emphatically, "Now Fred, it's all arranged. It's best this way, believe me."

"Just as you say, of course, my dear," he replied uncertainly. "All the same, I'd have thought—"

But nobody heard what he thought, as Susan called from above, "I hear the ambulance coming now." And she ran downstairs with her aunt's things.

"O.K. then, into the Land Rover quick, you three. We don't want to lose any time," he said. "I'll help the driver with your aunt, and then we'll follow the ambulance down to the main road, where I'll drop you off at your coach stop before going on down to the hospital."

"Oh, Fred, hadn't you better come back here straight after leaving the children?" objected Aunt Marian. "I'll be all right you know."

"No, no, I'd feel happier just to see you settled in. That won't take long. Then I'll come right back up here to see to the sheep. The coach stop is opposite the hospital entrance anyway."

The children were no sooner in the Land Rover than Susan peered in anxiously.

"What's the matter? Is . . . is Aunt Marian in awful pain?" faltered Anna.

Susan shook her head. "Oh no, the ambulance man and Uncle Fred are coping marvelously. It's all of you I'm fussed about. I only hope you'll be all right. Sure you're going to be warm enough?"

"Oh, Sue, we're absolutely boiling, and the coach will be like an oven. They always are, worse luck," said Verity, puffing out her cheeks in anticipation.

And Anna remarked, "We certainly won't be hungry, judging by the weight of this basket."

"Yes, you'll have plenty to eat, that's one good thing," agreed Susan. "I'd packed enough lunch for the four of us before I knew I wouldn't be coming with you."

"Then how can we help being all right?" laughed Verity. "We've only got to sit in a heated coach and eat and drink until we get home. And by that time the basket won't even be heavy to carry up to the house because we'll have eaten everything."

"Well, I hope not everything," said Susan, smiling for the first time, "because there'll still be the bacon and home-made yeast cake for Mummy. But now they're off, and here's Uncle Fred. So you're absolutely sure you'll be all right?"

"Of course we will, couldn't be righter," they chorused, waving at her through the swirling snow as the Land Rover followed the ambulance out of the yard.

"I'm jolly glad I'm not the eldest, always having to worry about the rest of the family," remarked Verity thoughtfully. "You won't start worrying, will you, Anna, even if you are the eldest for today?"

"Of course I won't, why ever should I?" said Anna gaily. But in spite of her cheerful words she shivered suddenly, and not entirely with cold.

3

THE long lane from the farm to the main road was a strange sight, one bank already white with driven snow, the other scarcely touched.

"It's the way this wind is blowing it. I reckon we're in for a regular blizzard," said Uncle Fred grimly. "Well, at any rate you kids will be all right, traveling into England. Your coach will run right out of it in an hour or so, most likely. We always seem to get the worst of it up here in the Welsh mountains."

"Well, at least Brian has seen what snow is like. It must be queer never to have seen it," said Verity.

The two vehicles slithered cautiously down the rutted lane, the ambulance going very slowly to avoid jolting Aunt Marian. When they eventually turned into the main road, they had to move more slowly still. There were no sheltering hedges here, and a treacherous white surface covered the road. They felt the Land Rover skid slightly, and Uncle Fred, always a cautious driver, gripped the wheel nervously, while the ambulance drew ahead.

"Don't want to lose sight of it if I can help it, or I might miss the hospital turning," he muttered, leaning forward in his seat to peer through the wedge-shaped slice of windshield that was all the snow-laden wipers could keep clear.

For a while the squeal of the wind and the muffled click-click of the wipers were the only sounds to be heard, until Anna remarked thoughtfully: "It seems rather a lonely place for a hospital, way out here on its own."

"Ah, it is that," agreed her uncle. "But there, I suppose they had this big old place standing empty—no sense letting it go to waste when we needed a hospital anyway. Ah, there she goes, turning off the main road now," he added, as the ambulance swung off the wide road and disappeared down a long avenue of trees.

"That must be our coach stop then," said Anna, pointing to a small shelter on the opposite side of the road.

"Hm, well, at least it's got a roof, so I suppose it will protect you from the snow if not the wind," remarked her uncle, looking with some disapproval at the drafty little hut. "Not many using it, I guess. I expect it's only here for the nurses, and an occasional hospital visitor maybe."

He drew up and looked at his watch. "Only fifteen minutes till the coach is due," he said. "I'd like to wait so you could sit in the Land Rover until it comes, but I must go down and see your aunt into the hospital. Anyhow, maybe I'll pass back before you've left—depends how long I'm kept at the hospital. And you'd best be jumping about to keep yourselves warm in this bitter-cold wind," he advised as he handed down their suitcases.

"We will," promised Verity, swinging the suitcase over her head as she started to dance up and down.

The three drew back into the shelter and watched the Land Rover creep across the road and into the hospital drive, where it was quickly blotted out by the whirling snow.

"Rather fun being on our own. It feels like being the only three people in the whole world," said Verity, dumping her suitcase beside the hut. "Uncle Fred was right about the cold, though. We really do need to keep moving," she went on jerkily, hopping from foot to foot and swinging her arms as she talked.

"Nothing very special about that, you're always moving anyway," commented Anna with an amused grin. But Verity did not hear. She had already hopped across to the entrance and was peering out.

"Mind you, this isn't really my favorite kind of snow," she remarked critically. "It looks all right on the ground, of course, but it seems so kind of busy, spinning down in such a hurry. I like quiet snow best, floating down in big, soft flakes like feathers."

"Well, this suits me," said Brian contentedly. "It looks just like the Christmas cards you send us every year. I never thought I'd be lucky enough to see it in real life. Of course we'd really hoped to get over here in time for Christmas, if Dad could have got away a few days sooner."

"Well, we didn't have a white Christmas this year anyway," said Anna. "Actually, we hardly ever do. We'd be more likely to have snow for Christmas if they'd kept to the old date."

"Old date? I didn't know there was ever any different date for Christmas," said Verity, much surprised.

"Oh yes, January 6 is Old Christmas Day."

"January 6—why, that's next Thursday," exclaimed Verity. "So you will see a white Christmas, Brian; that is, if our coach doesn't run right out of it, as Uncle Fred said it might. What do you do in Australia for Christmas, anyway?"

"Oh, we usually have a picnic on the beach. But I wanted to see a real English Christmas, with snow and a Christmas tree and candles."

"Well, you've got the snow all right, and I don't see why you shouldn't have the rest," cried Verity enthusiastically. "You'll be with us on Old Christmas Day, so why shouldn't we give you an old English Christmas? We can, can't we, Anna? We could bring out the Christmas tree again and the decorations—"

She broke off to step outside, her eye suddenly caught

by the snow covering every small unevenness on the windward side of the hut.

"It's such fine snow, you wouldn't believe it could build up as quickly as this," she said wonderingly, running her finger along the narrow window ledge and scooping up a little mound of snow.

"It's this wind. It's blowing it almost level," said Anna with a sudden shiver. "Come on. We'd better move our cases and things right inside. They're plastered with snow, even in this short time."

They shifted their suitcases and the basket into the shelter, lining them up along the wall below the window, out of reach of the snow that was driving in through the entrance.

"Do look. We've even got a snow door mat." Verity jumped across the smooth square of snow blown in through the unprotected doorway.

"You'd better move inside too, Brian. You're getting covered in snow yourself," advised Anna, catching Verity's eye with an amused wink. The boy was standing outside, lost in a dream as he gazed at the swirling snow.

"I don't want to waste one bit of it," he murmured, shuffling reluctantly backward into the hut.

"You look just like a snowman," said Verity, beating the worst of the snow off his shoulders. "I say, let's make a snowman while we're waiting!"

"Oh, Verity, there isn't time. Besides, this snow is far too wet," objected Anna.

"Well, snowballs then. It doesn't take a minute to make a snowball, and there's heaps of snow up there." She pointed to where the ground rose steeply behind the hut, the lower slope thickly wooded with small, straggling trees, their trunks already whitened down one side.

"Oh, be a sport!" she wheedled, noting Anna's hesitation. "You know Mummy did say we must show Brian as many of the special things of this country as possible while he's over here. And snow is a very special thing, and something he can never see at home."

"Well, don't go far," warned Anna, glancing at her watch. "You've only got ten minutes, remember."

At any other time Anna would have been first up the slope, relying on Susan to call her down when the coach was due. But now, as eldest, it was up to her to watch the time. She felt responsible for the luggage too, and shifted their suitcases still farther in from the doorway. What had started as a door mat of snow in the entrance was rapidly spreading over the floor in a widening carpet of white.

"This place is more of a snow trap than a shelter," she muttered, wiping snow off the top of the thermos flask with her sleeve. She heard the laughter of the other two, then a delighted squeal as the first icy snowball found its mark.

She looked at her watch for the third time. Six minutes to go. But suppose the coach was early? She decided to call the others. But when she went out she was surprised to see Brian standing alone on the wooded slope, shifting a half-made snowball from hand to hand as he looked about in bewilderment.

"Where's Verity?" she demanded sharply.

"I don't know," he said. "I just scooped up a new snowball, and when I turned around to throw it, she'd vanished."

"What do you mean, vanished? She can't have."

"Of course I haven't vanished. I'm here!" Verity's voice was muffled but indignant enough to prove that wherever she was, she clearly wasn't hurt.

"It's just that I can't get out of here," she went on in an aggrieved tone. "And more snow keeps falling in on top of me, so I can't see what I'm doing."

Anna scrambled up toward the spot where Brian was trying to push through a barrier of snow-covered bushes.

"Careful," she warned. "Don't you fall, too. There must be a pit or something here."

It was, in fact, an unused path, partially blocked by a fallen tree. Brambles and honeysuckle had climbed through the branches, and now the driving snow had overlaid the whole tangled mass until it seemed no more than another hump in the ground. However, a gaping hole in the whiteness showed where Verity had tumbled through.

Anna struggled through the snow and brambles until she reached this hole. Peering down, she saw Verity doubled across a stout branch, her dangling feet kicking frantically as they tried to find a foothold on the steep bank below.

"Sure you aren't hurt?" Anna questioned anxiously.

"No, but I tell you I can't get up," complained Verity as her foot skidded against the slippery bank.

"Here, give me your hand and I'll pull you up," said Anna, clinging to a branch with one hand and reaching down with the other. But Verity was heavier than she looked, and now that she was weighed down with boots and winter clothes, it took Anna's and Brian's combined efforts to haul her up.

"The trouble was, I stepped on a patch of snow that hadn't got anything under it," said Verity in an injured tone. "Anyone would have fallen through. It looked just as solid as all the rest."

"I only hope the rest is solid," said Anna nervously. "For goodness' sake, go carefully, both of you. Oh, help—I hope that isn't our coach!"

As she spoke, they all heard the ominous rumble, and a moment later the red-and-white coach came into view on the road below.

"Stop! Stop! STOP!" They yelled at the tops of their voices, leaping down through the undergrowth, forgetting all about possible pitfalls.

"They'll never hear us above this wind," panted Anna. But, unbelievably, the coach pulled up in front of the shelter as she spoke. She drew a breath of relief that was almost a sob, but in the same moment Verity let out a

despairing wail: "Oh, it's going on again without us!"

As the coach moved away, they saw that it had only stopped to put down a couple of young nurses, who ducked across the road and into a hospital bus waiting on the far side. A door slammed and the bus turned in through the hospital gates. A moment later another vehicle nosed out cautiously into the road.

"It's the Land Rover!" shouted Anna, wildly waving her arms. "Uncle Fred! Oh, Uncle Fred, wait—it's us, we're up here!"

But her voice was snatched away by the screaming wind, and the Land Rover swung into the road and was quickly lost to sight as it headed for home.

There was a moment's appalled silence, broken at last by Verity. "Why didn't he stop? He must have seen that our suitcases hadn't gone." She was very near to tears.

"He wouldn't be able to see our suitcases from the road. We'd dragged them inside, remember," Anna reminded her grimly. "He must have heard and seen the coach pull up at the shelter, so naturally he thinks we are safely inside it."

"How soon is the next coach?" asked Brian.

"Three o'clock—four hours from now," said Anna in a small voice.

Four hours! Verity drew a sobbing breath. It had been fun throwing snowballs for five minutes, but nobody could go on playing in this freezing wind for four hours.

They stumbled down toward the road without another word. The trees, small though they were, provided some protection, but when they stepped out onto the open road, they met the full force of the blizzard and were thankful to dodge back into the comparative shelter of the hut.

4

$\mathcal{W}$HATEVER can we do?" said Anna unsteadily. "I haven't seen a single thing come along this road except our Land Rover and the coach."

"Can't we go back to the f-f-farm?" asked Verity, whose teeth were beginning to chatter.

"We couldn't possibly walk all that way in this storm," said Anna. "It must be miles. It would take us simply ages, beating against the wind and snow."

"I wonder how far it is to the hospital," mused Brian. "If we followed the drive, we'd be bound to get there eventually. Anyhow, there just doesn't seem to be anywhere else." And he looked out over the desolate countryside, lying white and uninviting under the snow.

"What about the house up the hill behind us?" suggested Verity. "It's much nearer than the hospital."

"House? What house?" The other two swung around on her, and Anna said doubtfully, "I didn't see any house. Are you sure you didn't imagine it? Things look very different in the snow."

"Of course I didn't imagine it, I saw it—at least I saw chimneys and a bit of roof, so there must be a house."

"Well, we certainly can't stay here for four hours," decided Anna. "Just look how the snow has drifted in this short time. It's beginning to make quite a barrier across the entrance."

"Quick then, let's go before this whole doorway gets blocked up with snow so we can't get out," cried Verity, stepping hastily over the little wall of snow.

"It's perfectly all right—nothing in the world to worry about," said Anna, trying to copy the quiet, steadying tone with which Susan always calmed their excitable young sister.

The soothing words calmed her now, and she lifted her face to the snow with a smile, shutting her eyes against the spinning flakes.

But Anna's own fears were not so easily set at rest, and she longed for Susan's guidance as she and Brian picked up their luggage and followed Verity outside.

"I think that house of yours is a good idea," she went on, hoping her voice sounded as confident as Susan's. "Here, Verity, you'd better carry the suitcase. This basket's rather heavy."

Verity brushed the snow from her face and opened her

eyes. "I say, do look how the snow is collecting in little blobs in the hedge," she exclaimed, stepping forward to touch one with her finger and laughing delightedly as it collapsed in a sudden puff of white.

"Oh, come along, Verity, do, we haven't got all day," called Anna. "You've got to find the way to this house of yours, remember."

Verity liked hearing it called her house, and she started up the hill at a run. But the first few steps brought her stumbling to her knees.

"Goodness, it's getting quite deep," she panted as she picked herself up. "Our old footprints have been covered up already. You'd never guess anybody had been snowballing here at all."

"Well, whatever you do, don't fall into anything, either of you," cautioned Anna, struggling after her.

Even in this brief space of time, the snow had deepened under the trees, making it a good deal more difficult to walk than before, and they battled up the steep slope in silence, pausing often to catch their breath in the piercing air, and shifting their suitcases from one numbed hand to the other.

"Lucky it will still be daylight when it's time to come down for the coach," said Anna. "I'd hate to try and find the way down this hill in the dark."

They plodded slowly up through the trees, Verity first, then Anna, and finally Brian, who dropped farther behind at every step as he kept stopping to look about him.

The driving snow made it impossible to see more than a few yards ahead, and Anna was growing anxious when Verity suddenly called out in triumph: "There it is!"

The other two struggled up to where she stood, and saw the dim outline of a huddle of gray stone buildings.

"That looks like a barn at the end, so I expect it is a farm," said Anna in relief. The sight of a human habitation put new heart into them all, and they hurried forward until they were on a level with the house.

"This must be the back. I can't see a gate," called Verity leading the way. "Never mind. Here's a gap where the wall is falling down a bit—we'll be able to get into the yard through here."

"It looks awfully shabby and tumbledown, though," she called back doubtfully as she neared the house.

"We'll probably find they're quite poor people, living in a lonely place like this, without a proper road," said Anna. "But that's not likely to stop them inviting us inside."

"I hope they haven't got lots of fierce farm dogs," said Verity, looking about her nervously as they crossed the silent yard.

"If they've got any sense, they'll be sheltering in some shed on a day like this," said Anna. "Even the hens aren't pecking about the place today."

"I think the entrance must be around the other side," she went on. "It looks as though they aren't using this side of the house at all."

But when they got around to the front, they found it as blank as the back.

"Oh dear, it looks as though they're out," cried Verity.

"I'm afraid the house is empty," said Anna very quietly.

"Empty?" echoed Verity in dismay. "Oh, I did so want a fire." Her teeth began chattering again, and she seemed to shrink in size as she huddled into her anorak.

Brian pressed his face against an uncurtained window. "I'm afraid you're right," he agreed. "There's no furniture in this room, anyhow—just a pile of broken boxes, and the paper peeling off the wall in strips."

"And the door is locked," said Anna, trying the handle.

Verity pressed hard against the doorpost, trying to control her shivering, while the snow piled up on the hood of her anorak making it look like a white fur cap.

"Well, even if the place is empty, I don't see why we shouldn't shelter inside," said Brian.

"If we could get inside," said Anna, looking up at the closed windows.

"Oh, there'll probably be a loose window we can force open somewhere in a crumbling old house like this," he answered cheerfully. "I'll go and have a look." And he disappeared around the side of the house.

He was soon back. "There's another door, but that's locked too," he told them. "But I've found a hopeful-looking window opening into a sort of pantry place with

stone slabs for shelves. I managed to work it up a bit. I can only raise it about six inches, but I think Verity might be small enough to wriggle through. Then she can open the door and let us in."

He led them around to the back of the house and pointed to a small window set low in the thick wall.

"Think you could squeeze through there, Verity?"

"I might if I take off a few clothes," she said, peeling off her raincoat and anorak.

Even without her extra clothes, Verity found it a tight squeeze, but this house was her discovery and she was determined to be the first to get inside.

"Don't get stuck, whatever you do," warned Anna. However, once her head and shoulders were through, Verity was able to catch hold of a stone shelf and pull herself inside. As she slid to the floor, the others let the window fall shut behind her with a clatter, and for one moment she savored the thrill of being the only living person in the deserted house. Then the others began to batter on the door, calling to her to hurry up, while the howling wind reminded her of the bitter cold outside. She ran to the door but found it locked.

"Try the other door then. There must be a key in one of them. We'll run around," called Anna.

The front door was bolted but not locked, and although her fingers were stiff with cold, Verity managed to slide back the bolts and drag the door open.

The others pushed in thankfully, stamping their snow-caked boots and shaking showers of snow from their clothes, while Verity slammed the heavy door behind them and bolted it against the buffeting wind.

Opposite the room that Brian had seen through the window, there was another larger room across the passage.

"Ah, this is better. This must have been the kitchen," said Anna, looking across at the vast black range that filled most of one wall. Beyond it was a deep recess.

"It looks like a cupboard, except that it hasn't got any shelves," said Verity, peering in.

"I know—I bet I know what it is," cried Anna. "It's an old box bed."

"A box bed? Why box? And why downstairs in the kitchen?" Verity wanted to know.

"I don't know why, but I know they used to build beds into walls like this. Sometimes they had sliding doors or curtains to shut them off from the room."

"Must have been cozy when the fire was alight," mused Verity. "I wouldn't mind a bit being the first to go to bed if I could lie in there all evening with the rest of the family sitting around the fire."

"I don't imagine that would have been the children's bed," said Anna. "Much more likely to have been for the parents, while the children slept upstairs."

"Poor things—how cold for them," murmured Verity with a little shiver which Anna was quick to notice.

"Look here, let's eat our picnic now. That will warm

us up," she suggested. "We could even sit in the box bed to eat it. The wooden boards wouldn't be nearly as cold as this drafty old stone floor."

She got the basket and they all climbed into the cupboard-like space, huddling together for warmth.

"Oh, I say, hard-boiled eggs *and* cheese sandwiches! Good old Sue, she's given us a real feast," said Verity happily as she cracked her eggshell against the wooden partition.

There were Welsh cakes too, and bananas, and best of all, a large thermos bottle of steaming hot chocolate.

"That's warmed me right down to the very ends of my toes and fingers. Almost as good as a fire," declared Verity, putting down her empty mug with a contented sigh. Her last words gave Anna an idea.

"I don't see why we shouldn't light a fire in this grate, since we've got to stay here for several hours," she said. "We could burn all those old boxes for a start."

"What if the owners suddenly come back?" asked Verity apprehensively.

"I don't believe they are coming back," said Anna slowly. "By the look of the place, I'd say it's been empty for years. Anyway, let's hunt around and see if we can find enough wood to make a really good fire. Then we— oh!" She broke off with a sudden gasp, clapping her hand to her mouth as she stared from one to the other. "But I quite forgot, we haven't any matches."

"I have," said Brian placidly, and putting his hand in

his pocket, he brought out a souvenir book of matches.

"They gave these away on the plane coming over," he explained. "We'll have to go easy with them, though. There aren't an awful lot."

"Enough for one fire," said Anna happily. "Come on, let's go and look for firewood."

5

ROM the kitchen a door opened into a long, raftered building with a row of wooden mangers along one wall.

"The cowhouse," commented Anna. "This must be one of the old Welsh long-houses Aunt Marian was telling us about. You remember, she said they had the cattle shed under the same roof as the dwelling house, so that they could see to the animals in winter without having to go outside."

"Good idea," said Verity, glancing out at the scudding snow.

"Not quite such a good idea as you'd think," said Anna. "Aunt Marian's farm used to be like that, but Grandfather blocked up the connecting door when she was a child because Granny couldn't stand the smell of cows in the kitchen."

"Oof—I never thought of that," said Verity, wrinkling up her nose in disgust.

Brian had wandered through to the far end of the shed and he now called from the shadows: "I say, there's quite a bit of coal down here, and any amount of wood. So we can have our fire all right."

"Coal?" said Anna doubtfully. "I wonder if we ought to touch that? It doesn't seem quite the same as using wood, somehow."

"Well, nobody's touched this coal for years, that's certain. It's covered in dust and matted cobwebs," he assured her. "I don't suppose anyone even remembers it's here. In any case, I can't believe anybody would grudge us a fire on a freezing day like this."

"You're right, of course they wouldn't . . . if indeed they ever come back at all," murmured Anna. She looked out across the snowy yard, then took a quick step toward the window.

"I say, just look, I'm sure that must be a well out there," she exclaimed in surprise, pointing to a rounded wall topped by winch and handle. There was even a dented bucket attached to the chain. It was mounded now with snow, but clearly intended for use.

"A well! Oh, I must go out and see," cried Verity, darting toward the door. But Anna caught her back.

"Oh no you don't," she said emphatically. "One slip

in this snow and you might fall in, and we'd never be able to get you out. It's sure to be frightfully deep."

"I only wanted to see," protested Verity.

"We'll all go out, but we'll go together," said Anna firmly. "But first let's get the fire going. I'm just aching with cold."

Verity discovered that she was shivering again, and suddenly a fire seemed more important than anything else.

Brian was busy poking about in the coal. "I've found an old bucket," he reported. "It's full of holes, but better than nothing. Let's take in some of these branches too. We'll have to break them up as best we can. I can't see a chopper anywhere."

The two girls dragged branches and larger chunks of wood into the kitchen, while Brian followed with a bucket of coal. He was right about the holes. A black trail of coal dust trickled across the floor behind him as he walked.

"I do wish we had a bit more paper," said Anna, smoothing out the flimsy bags in which their sandwiches had been packed.

"Don't forget those boxes next door. They'll make splendid kindling," Brian reminded her. He went and got a couple of the boxes and broke them into slim strips, which he laid carefully over the crumpled paper bags that Anna had arranged in the grate.

"Leave plenty of space for air to circulate," she ad-

vised. "And better go easy with that coal. Small knobs will catch best at the start. I only hope the wood is really dry."

"Can I light it?" begged Verity, edging nearer.

"All right. Only wait till we've finished laying it. We've got to try and make certain it catches the first time, because there's no more paper, once these bags are burnt."

"And mind you don't let the match go out," warned Brian as he handed over the precious book.

The match did not go out and the flame was soon licking eagerly at the paper, sending out fresh little spurts to catch first in one spot, then in another. A thin coil of smoke appeared, and Anna held her breath as she watched it twisting lazily among the little sticks. Then suddenly she heard the crackle she was waiting for.

"Ah—it's catching!" she whispered in relief.

Nevertheless, she continued to hover apprehensively around the fireplace, feeding the flames with slivers of wood and later with little pieces of coal. It was fifteen minutes or more before she was satisfied that it was safely caught and ready to be heaped with larger lumps of coal and wood.

They all continued to stand around the fire, not because it needed watching any longer, but because it was so good to feel their numbed fingers beginning to tingle in the warmth.

Verity was no sooner warm than she remembered the well. "Do let's go out and look at it now," she begged.

"Pull up the hood of your anorak then, and button your raincoat," said Anna. "Not that it matters so much if we do get wet now we've got this gorgeous fire to dry our things."

She was very particular about approaching the well, however, and took a tight hold on Brian's coat as he leaned over the low wall.

"Can't see any water at all," he said. "It must be a long way down."

He shoved a pile of snow off the rim of the well and a few seconds later they heard a splash as it hit the water far below.

"Deep enough, anyway," he remarked. "I'll let down the bucket."

"Mind you don't slip," cried Anna nervously. "Here, help me hang on to him, Verity."

Brian shook the snow from the bucket. Then, making sure it was properly attached to the chain, he lowered it into the well. They heard a muffled splash as it struck the water, then the chain grew taut as it filled and sank. He began to turn the wooden handle, and as he did so, drips from the swinging bucket echoed eerily from the depths.

"What beautiful clear water!" exclaimed Anna when the brimming bucket reached the top.

"Might as well take it indoors now that we've got it," said Brian, slipping the hook from the handle and swinging the bucket to the ground.

One bucketful was enough for the moment, and even

Verity was thankful to run back to the house and into the warmth of the firelit kitchen.

"How cozy this is," she said contentedly, turning her hands in the firelight, so that first one side and then the other felt the warmth. "How long have we got before we have to leave here?"

Anna looked at her watch. "It's just after one o'clock now and the coach leaves at three. Say we allow half an hour to walk down to the shelter. That gives us about another hour and a half up here."

"Good!" said Verity happily. "I like this place. It feels like having a home of our very own, doesn't it?"

"Yes," said Anna, looking around the homey, old-fashioned room. "It's got a friendly, welcoming feel about it, somehow. It's easy to picture those shelves full of pretty china and great sides of home-cured bacon hanging from the ceiling."

"And a family just like us all sitting around the fire," finished Verity.

"I do just wish I could make us all a hot drink before we leave," said Anna, looking longingly at the iron hook dangling over the fire.

"Come to think of it, I saw an old black caldron in that washhouse place at the back," said Brian. "I'll go and see if it's any good."

He was gone some time, and when he returned, the caldron swung from his hand, wet and shining.

"I've washed it out with lots of snow," he explained.

"And then I rinsed it with water from the bucket to test it for holes. It seems to be perfectly sound."

The hook and chain hung from a hinged iron bar fitted into the chimney above the range. They swung this forward and lifted the caldron of water onto the hook, then swung it back over the fire, where the leaping flames were soon licking its black sides.

"It looks more like a picture book than real life," remarked Verity. "Much more exciting than an electric kettle."

"Now all we need is something to sit on," said Anna. "It would be just wonderful to be able to draw up our chairs to the fire as in a real home. But there doesn't seem to be any furniture in the house."

"There might be something in the sheds that we could use," suggested Brian. "I'll go and have a look."

"I'll come too," cried Verity, glad of an excuse to be on the move again.

They soon returned in triumph, carrying a long bench between them.

"Do look. The seat is simply made of a tree trunk split down the middle, but it stands as steady as anything—just you try," said Verity as they set the bench down in front of the fire.

"I don't understand this set-up at all," said Brian with a puzzled frown. "You can see this house has been empty for years, and yet there are masses of hay in the barn, and a great heap of swedes—or perhaps they're turnips—that must have been dug up this year, by the look of them."

"I expect when the last people left this place nobody else wanted to come and live here. Lots of people would find it far too lonely," said Anna. "But of course the land would still be useful for crops and grazing. So perhaps someone is just using the land and outbuildings, while leaving the poor old house to crumble away. What a waste it seems, though. It would make such a lovely home."

For a while they sat in silence, watching the flames leap under the hanging caldron, while the wind howled around the house and an occasional snowflake drifted down the wide chimney to hiss into the fire.

6

VERITY could never keep still for long, and as soon as she was warm all through, she was on her feet again.

"What now, you restless thing?" asked Anna, laughing.

"I'm just going to see what it's like upstairs," replied Verity. When they first came in, she had noticed the wide stone staircase curving up from the passage, and she now went up to explore.

There was no landing at the top, not even a door. The stairs just led straight into the queerest bedroom she had ever seen. It stretched the full length of the house under the ragged thatch, which sloped right down to the floor on either side. The long room was divided by the massive bulk of the chimney, which thrust up through the floor, rising in three great steps to the roof above. At the far end of the room a tiny, one-paned window peeped out through the thick wall on a level with the floor.

She wanted to linger and poke about, but already the biting wind was turning her feet and hands to ice, and she was drawn back against her will to the warmth of the room below.

As she went into the kitchen, she found it surprisingly darker than the bedroom. Glancing toward the window, she saw the reason.

"I say, just look at the snow now. It's reached halfway up the window," she exclaimed with a little shiver of uneasiness. There was something frightening about snow that piled up as fast as that.

Anna swung around on her seat by the fire and stared at the window in silence for a long moment. Then she got up and went out of the room.

She was soon back, shaking the snow from her raincoat and stamping her boots until scattered blobs of snow lay melting on the floor all around her. Her face was very white and her voice unsteady when she spoke.

"I've just never seen anything like the way it's drifting," she said shakily. "It's halfway up the back door, and that broken wall where we climbed in has completely disappeared. There's not even a ridge in the snow to show where it is."

The other two stared at her, not grasping what this meant, until she went on: "I don't see how we can ever get down to the road in this."

"Not get down? But we've got to." Brian's voice was calmly matter-of-fact as he made for the door. But when he pulled it open, he let out a long whistle of surprise.

"I say, I never knew snow could be like this," he murmured in an awed tone.

Verity joined him on the doorstep, staring silently into the whirling whiteness.

"All the same, we ought to be able to find the way, even without the wall to guide us," said Brian. "I remember that shed over there for a start. I know we came past that."

"Yes, I remember that too," put in Verity eagerly. "And there were some pigsties too, only . . ." She halted doubtfully. "Only they seem to have vanished, same as the wall. I suppose they're buried too."

"Anyway, let's go out and do a bit of prospecting," suggested Brian, struggling into his raincoat.

But once they rounded the corner of the house they met the full force of the blizzard and there was no more talking.

Brian led the way, his eyes half closed against the blinding snow which was driving horizontally across the open yard. Anna stumbled after him, her hood pulled low over her forehead to protect it from the aching cold. Verity struggled along beside her for a while, but at last, unable to endure the snow in her face any longer, she turned her back on the storm and shuffled along behind them, walking backward in their tracks.

When they eventually reached the far side of the yard, Brian plunged up to his waist in drifted snow, trying to force his way through to where he knew the hidden wall must be.

Anna turned her back for a moment to catch her breath and saw Verity's snow-plastered figure staggering along behind her.

"It's no good, Brian. We can't go on," she decided. "We aren't even out of the farmyard yet, and already Verity looks like a snowman."

"I f-f-feel like a snowman too, a . . . a . . . a—*tchoo*—a sneezing snowman," exploded Verity.

"Come along, back to the fire," ordered Anna, seizing her by the hand.

With the driving wind behind them, they soon floundered back to the house and burst panting into the kitchen. But although their snow-wet faces burned in the sudden warmth, their frozen hands were so numb with cold that it was all they could do to fumble off their snow-caked coats and anoraks.

"So what now?" asked Brian, staring in surprise at his own hands, blotched and reddened with cold.

"I'm afraid we'll have to stay here for the night," said Anna quietly.

"For the night?" repeated Verity incredulously. "But where can we sleep?"

"There's the box bed," said Anna.

"And plenty of hay in the barn," said Brian. "We're lucky to have that in this cold weather."

"But what about supper . . . and breakfast?" demanded Verity.

"We've got Aunt Marian's cake," Anna reminded her. "And of course there's the bacon, too, whether we like it or not."

She stood for a moment trying to imagine what Susan would do. Then she caught Verity watching her anxiously and remembered that she was the eldest. Whatever happened, she must not let the others guess that she was worried.

"Well, first we'd better collect some hay for the night," she said cheerfully, turning toward the door. "And we'll need to get in plenty of coal and wood. And water too," she added. "We won't be able to do a thing once it begins to get dark."

For the next hour they were so busy that even Anna had no time to worry about anything beyond the job in hand.

They carried in great armfuls of hay, spreading a foot-deep layer in the box bed.

"Doesn't it smell gorgeous?" said Verity, taking a deep breath. "It looks cozy too. I'm even beginning to look forward to bedtime."

They searched the house and outbuildings for anything in the way of cans and jars and boxes. They filled undamaged jars and cans with water from the well, and put coal into anything that would not hold water. The wood they stacked around the walls of the kitchen.

"It seems an awful lot of wood for one fire," remarked Verity, pausing to rest her aching arms.

"I know," said Anna. "But we'll need to keep the fire going all night long or we'll be frozen. We'll have to sit up in turns to look after it."

"Night watches, like nurses do—what fun!" said Verity. Mention of nurses turned her thoughts in a new direction, and she went on: "I say, wouldn't Aunt Marian be surprised if she could see us now! I wonder if Uncle Fred guessed we missed that coach?"

"Of course he didn't or he'd have waited for us," said Anna. "He naturally thinks we got in when it stopped at the shelter. And Mummy is not expecting us till Friday —which is jolly lucky, as it happens."

"So nobody's worried about us," said Verity. "Except you," she went on, studying her sister's face. "Poor Anna, that's the worst of being the eldest."

"Oh, I'm not worried now, not really," said Anna hastily. "Why should I be? We've got a house and a fire and bedding and enough food for supper and breakfast. And we'd better have our supper now," she finished, glancing toward the dim square of window. "It's beginning to get dark already."

Verity looked unenthusiastically at the cold boiled bacon as Anna took it out of its wrappings.

"I think I'll just have cake," she decided. "What are we going to have to drink?"

"There's nothing we can have but water, and that will have to be boiled."

"Why? I'd rather have it cold—it looked so lovely and clear in the bucket."

"It did, and it's probably perfectly pure. There are no taps in the house, so they must have drunk it themselves. All the same, I'd rather boil it and be on the safe side."

Verity sighed. The meal sounded dreadfully dull, and she happened to be especially hungry. She stood watching Anna hack jagged chunks of bacon off the joint with the only knife they'd been able to find, a blunt old thing with a broken blade that looked as though it might have been used for digging up weeds.

"It would hardly cut butter—no wonder they left it behind," muttered Anna as she sawed away at the meat. She arranged the clumsy slices on broken slates.

"They are all I can find to use as plates," she explained. "Not quite as nice as Aunt Marian's 'Remember me' plates, I'm afraid!"

Verity giggled, remarking as she passed a slateful of bacon to Brian: "This will be a meal to tell them about when you get back to Australia!"

"Home life in Wales!" said Anna, laughing.

"And this really is our home for tonight," said Verity, settling down happily on the bench by the fire.

They decided to do their fire watches for an hour at a time, taking turns.

"I'll put my wristwatch here on the windowsill so each of us can time ourselves," said Anna.

"And you faithfully promise you'll wake me, won't you, so I can take fair turns with you both?" insisted Verity, determined not to be allowed to go on sleeping, just because she happened to be the youngest.

She climbed into the box bed and snuggled happily into the hay, while Brian rustled around in a corner where he had built himself an elaborate bed of piled hay, hedged around with boxes.

Anna settled down on the bench by the fire to take the first watch.

7

*T*HE first part of the night was fun as they took turns looking after the fire. They heaped on coal and sticks until the flames leaped roaring up the chimney, filling the bare old room with dancing light, which helped them to forget the snow piling up around the house outside.

But as the night wore on, they found it more and more difficult to keep awake, and from time to time one or another of them nodded off to sleep, only to jerk awake with a sudden start, feeling stiff and guilty.

Anna could scarcely believe it was her turn again already when Verity shook her awake for yet another watch. So she was surprised to learn that she had, in fact, had a longer sleep than usual.

"I'm afraid I've been a bit more than an hour this

time, but I kept falling asleep. I simply couldn't help it," confessed Verity, climbing drowsily into the box bed as Anna crawled out, still more than half asleep.

"Never mind. You've kept up a grand fire, and that's what matters." She yawned, stumbling toward the bench.

There was no reply from the box bed. Verity was deep in the hay and fast asleep already.

Anna could never remember how she reached the bench, or whether indeed she sat on it at all. She remembered nothing until a falling cinder startled her awake and she found herself lying curled on her raincoat in front of the hearth. She knew she must have slept for a long time, for the room was filled with feeble daylight.

She scrambled to her feet and ran to the window to see if it had stopped snowing. The glass appeared to be misted over and she rubbed a cold pane with her hand. But no clear patch appeared, and leaning closer, she realized she was looking out into solid snow. With a sudden little prickle of fear, she ran to the front door and wrenched it open.

Now she was really frightened, for although a quantity of loosened snow fell in when she opened the door, it made no difference to the snow piled up outside. The doorway was completely blocked, and she found herself staring up at a solid wall of whiteness.

In a panic she stepped forward and plunged her arms into it up to the elbow, but no matter how much she scooped away, there was always more beyond.

She wondered fearfully if the house was completely buried, and if so, how they would ever escape. Could people breathe under snow, she wondered. She was almost afraid to put this fear to the test, but she forced herself to take a deep breath. The air was so piercingly cold that it made her sneeze, but at least it proved there was something to breathe!

Feeling in desperate need of companionship, she called to the others. But they slept on, and she was too frightened to waste time on them. Without troubling to shut the door, she ran down the length of the cowhouse to the door at the far end. It was a half door, and when she finally managed to pull the top half open, she was confronted by another wall of snow.

For a moment she could only stand there, gripping the lower half of the door until her knuckles whitened. Then, pulling herself together, she flew back through the cowhouse to find Brian standing half awake in the kitchen doorway.

"What's up?" he asked, startled by her expression.

"I don't know. Oh, Brian, I just don't know," she cried, fighting back tears of rising panic. "I'm afraid we may be completely buried in snow. Could we be, do you think?"

"Haven't a clue. I don't know about snow," he replied with his usual calm. "How about going upstairs? Then we can at least see if it's up as high as the bedroom window."

"Good idea," she said gratefully, steadied at once by his calmness. "Quiet, though," she added in a whisper. "We may as well let Verity sleep on. No point scaring her before we need to."

They found the tiny floor-level window coated in blown snow, but when Brian forced it open, the snow slid off the single pane and they looked out into empty space. The effect was almost as unexpected as the wall of snow had been.

"It's not just like another country, it's like another world," marveled Brian.

Anna could find no words at all. She simply knelt on the floor in front of the little window and stared and stared. It had stopped snowing, and the early light revealed an unbroken waste of snow stretching away as far as they could see.

There were no trees on this side of the house, and lesser objects such as gates and hedges had been completely covered, without leaving the least unevenness in the smooth whiteness.

"So we really are buried, almost up to the level of this upstairs window," she murmured at last.

"If the sun breaks through later on, then perhaps the warmth will melt it," suggested Brian hopefully. "Or how about throwing buckets of hot water out the front door. Wouldn't that melt a passage through the snow?"

Anna said nothing. It wasn't as though they had to clear a way only into the yard. It would take more water than they could boil in a week to clear a track down to the road and other people. And other people were what she wanted now, more than anything else in the world. There was something very lonely about being the eldest and the only one responsible for a younger sister and an unrealistic dreamer like Brian, however clever he might be.

She closed the little window and got to her feet, realizing that any practical suggestions must come from her.

"We must shut those doors downstairs for a start, and keep the house warm," she said, making for the stairs.

"I suppose I may as well see how I get on with digging, before we bother with boiling water," mused Brian, following her out of the room. "I'd better clear a path to the well first of all—although we've enough water left for breakfast, haven't we?"

The mention of breakfast alarmed Anna. They had eaten most of the cake for supper, and she wondered how long the bacon would last, even if nobody liked it much.

They returned to the kitchen and she heaped more wood on the fire, not only for warmth but also for light, since little daylight penetrated the snow-blocked window. The fire was reassuring too, and as the dancing flames lit up the simple room, Anna felt strangely comforted, sensing the protection of the kindly house as a core of warmth and safety at the heart of a frozen world.

Verity stirred and sat up in the box bed, sleepily brushing hay from her tangled hair.

"You look like a little animal waking up from its winter sleep," laughed Brian. "But you've woken too soon, little animal. It's not spring yet, by a long way. We're slap in the middle of the most tremendous winter you ever saw. Do you know, we are actually buried in snow, right over the doors and almost up to the roof?"

"B-b-buried?" Verity's eyes darted to Anna's face in alarm.

"It's going to be absolutely all right," Anna assured her quickly, while Brian picked up his shovel and announced: "Anyway, I'm off now to start digging us out."

Verity glanced uncertainly from one to the other, until Anna's smile reassured her and she said: "This seems to be turning into a pretty exciting adventure, but a nice one too." And she scrambled out of bed.

"You're right about the adventure," called Brian. "Just come and look at this." And he beckoned her across to the snow-blocked doorway.

"There you are—walled in by snow!" he said gleefully.

"But how will we ever get out?" she began, her anxiety threatening to return.

"I'm going to dig a tunnel through to the yard for a start," he told her.

"A tunnel? Oh, can I help?"

"Better come and have breakfast first. The water's boiling," called Anna from the kitchen.

This time Verity did not ask what they were going to have. Instead, she fetched their picnic mugs and waited for Anna to fill them with hot water from the caldron.

"You'd never guess hot water could look so tempting," she remarked, watching the steam drift away from the mugs in her hands. She stood them in front of the fire, then returned to stand with a slate plate in each hand while Anna hacked at the bacon with the blunt old knife. Soon they were sitting in a row on the bench, eating ragged chunks of cold boiled bacon with their fingers.

"I bet this is nicer than what explorers get on Arctic expeditions," remarked Brian, licking his fingers appreciatively.

"And Arctic explorers certainly don't have a fire like this," said Anna, smiling.

"Or a box bed full of hay," said Verity. "And do you know a funny thing?" she finished. "I find I like home-cured bacon better than I thought I did." And she wiped her greasy fingers on her slacks.

"I'll do the washing up!" said Anna, laughing as she collected slates and mugs.

"And I'll make the beds!" cried Verity, leaning into the box bed to stir and toss the hay.

Brian hurried off to the front door, and presently they heard the steady scrape and clank of his shovel as he started to scoop through the snow on the doorstep. It was soft and loosely piled and it was not long before he broke through into the open air.

"I say, come and look at it here," he called excitedly. "It's absolutely fantastic on this side of the house."

They ran to join him and stood peering through the opening he had made. It was indeed fantastic. The snow was not so evenly spread out here in the yard, where the house and outbuildings had broken the full force of the wind, allowing the snow to drift roof-high in places, while elsewhere it lay no more than a few feet deep. But the wind had played extraordinary tricks, whisking the snow into waves and eddies until it looked like elaborate frosting on some giant's Christmas cake. The upper parts of the house and barn rose starkly out of the whiteness, while a tree, top-heavy with snow, leaned over the buried gate.

"There's the well, anyway," said Brian, pointing to a huge hump in the snow. "I'll soon clear a path to that."

"I'll help. We've done the beds and washing up," said Verity. "I'll get the little coal shovel from the kitchen— all right, I'll bring it back, I promise," she added hastily, catching Anna's eye.

Together the shovels sounded terrific.

"Just like a whole gang of workmen building a road," said Verity. "You know, Brian, you're awfully lucky," she went on, "because you aren't just seeing an ordinary English winter, but something much more extra-special. We hardly ever get snow as deep as this, even here in Wales."

She was interrupted by Anna, who appeared in the doorway behind them. She had one of the swedes from the barn in her hand.

"I don't know whether these things are swedes or turnips or even mangel-wurzels," she said uncertainly. "But, whichever they are, I'm sure they're all right for humans to eat. So that will at least give us a change of food."

Verity said nothing. She loathed swedes and had never even heard of mangel-wurzels. She bent again to her digging, reminding herself that she was in the middle of an adventure and that real-life adventurers had to be prepared to put up with dull food as well as danger and excitement.

8

$\mathcal{W}$HEN Verity next went into the kitchen to warm her hands, she found Anna hacking the swede to pieces with the broken knife.

"What a lucky thing you learn cooking at school," she remarked admiringly. "I wouldn't a bit know what to do."

Anna laughed, remembering the spotless electric cookers and gleaming equipment in the school kitchens.

"Well, it's very different there, of course, with things like flour and butter," she explained. "And salt," she added regretfully, dropping the jagged pieces of swede into the caldron. "Miss Baker is very particular about salt. And as to what she'd say about this smoke . . ." She broke off to step back, blinking rapidly as the smoke stung tears into her smarting eyes.

"Oh, but I like the smell of smoke," said Verity,

sniffing appreciatively. "I wouldn't be a bit surprised if a smokey taste would be better than salt, with swedes."

"Perhaps I've invented a new way of cooking them—smoked swedes or kippered mangel-wurzels!" giggled Anna, wiping her streaming eyes on her sleeve.

"Then I expect they'll ask you to do a demonstration on TV, like that man we saw tossing pancakes!" laughed Verity, as she picked up her shovel and skipped away to rejoin Brian in the yard.

Anna joined them later, digging most successfully with half a broken slate. But she was really more concerned with her cooking, and kept slipping indoors to prod the swede with a stick. When she was satisfied that it wasn't going to get any softer, she fished the pieces out of the caldron. They had turned a nice bright yellow, but even so, they didn't look very exciting. She wished she had a fork so that she could mash them, and she longed for salt and butter to disguise the flavor. With a little sigh, she called the others.

They drew up to the fire with their slates balanced on their knees. On each slate was a slab of steaming swede and a small piece of cold bacon.

Verity eyed her swede suspiciously and started on the bacon. After a couple of mouthfuls she turned to Anna to say in surprise: "This bacon gets nicer and nicer. Are we allowed second helpings?"

"Better not," said Anna, "or it will be swede only for the next meal."

Verity was about to ask how many more meals they were having here, but something in Anna's strained expression prompted her to say, instead: "Aunt Marian couldn't call us fussy town children now, could she?"

"I can't imagine what she'd call us," said Anna, smiling at her young sister's determined expression as she concentrated on biting the last scrap of fat from the bacon rind she held in her grubby fingers.

When the brief meal was finished, they were tempted to linger on by the fire, but Anna got resolutely to her feet.

"Better get on. We've lots to do before dark," she reminded them, zipping up her anorak.

"Are we going to be here for another night then?" asked Verity.

"Looks like it, doesn't it?" muttered Brian, shouldering his shovel and leading the way outside.

Between them they cleared a path to the well and a space in front of it.

"Now we'd better fill every single thing we've got with water, in case this all gets snowed over again tonight," advised Anna.

"May I let down the bucket this time?" begged Verity.

"Wait then, while we hold you," ordered Anna, taking a firm grip on her raincoat.

Verity lowered the bucket into the black depths, listening for the splash and gurgle as it hit the water and sank. But she soon found that winding it up was more than she could manage alone, and Brian had to help her turn the handle until the brimming bucket came to the top, water slopping over its side.

They filled all the containers they had collected, carrying them carefully back to the house, where they lined them up along the kitchen wall. It was a chilly business, and on every trip they paused to warm their numbed hands in front of the fire before returning to the well.

"We really are working for our living, aren't we?" commented Verity.

When everything else was full, Brian fetched the caldron. Anna insisted on rinsing it out with several lots of clean water, to wash away the taste of swede before refilling it.

"I'll help you carry it back to the house. It's too heavy for you alone," said Brian. He and Anna carried it indoors between them and slung it on its hook above the fire.

When Anna returned to shut the outer door, Verity was still standing beside the well where they had left her.

"You can come along in now. We've got all the water we need," Anna called.

But, to her surprise, Verity flapped a hand, signaling her to be quiet.

"Whatever is it?" whispered Anna, tiptoeing out to join her.

"I don't know exactly, but I thought I heard a little

sort of smothered cry. It seemed to come from some-where over there beside the barn."

"The wind, most probably," said Anna uneasily as a sudden gust swept a little cloud of snow from the roof. "Anyway, come along in and get warm now. You're shivering," she urged, her voice taking on a sudden edge as a snowflake drifted by. She hoped Verity would not notice it, but she pulled up short on the doorstep to ex-claim: "Oh, Anna, look, it's starting to snow again."

"Then let's go and build up a monstrous fire," cried Anna, hustling her inside.

They went along to the end of the cowhouse and fetched wood and coal, heaping up the fire until the flames roared up the chimney, almost obscuring the old black caldron.

"I do believe it's starting to sing already," asserted Verity.

"Oh, come off it. It can't be even humming yet. You're always a hop ahead," teased Brian.

"Well, at least its clearing its throat, getting ready to hum!" laughed Verity. "Is it tea time yet?"

Anna looked at her watch, then held it to her ear. "Oh bother, it's stopped. I forgot to wind it," she exclaimed.

"Why worry?" said Brian tranquilly. "Time doesn't really make all that difference up here. We've just got light and dark, that's all. And as we've got no lamps or candles, we've jolly well got to do everything while the daylight lasts."

"Except look after the fire," Verity reminded him.

"Anyway, it's no good talking about a meal until I've cooked it," Anna pointed out. "I'm going to boil several swedes this time. Then there'll be some left over. Who knows?" she went on with a sudden grin. "Somebody might be glad of a little snack on night watch!"

Verity laughed and exclaimed: "I bet I'd be the only person in my form ever to have a midnight feast of cold swedes."

"They'll be iced swedes by midnight—nicer still," said Brian.

"Anyway, I'm sure nobody in my whole school has ever been in a real adventure where they could easily starve to death," she finished in a satisfied tone.

"Oh, Verity, don't say such things, even in fun," begged Anna.

"Ah, but you see, I know you won't really let us starve," replied Verity trustfully.

"Well, I'd better go along to the barn and get some swedes," said Anna, wishing she could feel as confident as her sister.

As she left the room, Brian got to his feet and strolled toward the door.

"Where are you going?" asked Verity curiously.

"I want to have a look at that bedroom," he replied. "I think I may have the beginnings of an idea."

"An idea? What is it? Oh, please tell," she cried eagerly.

But Brian merely shook his head. "The beginnings of an idea, I said. There's nothing yet worth telling."

She clenched her teeth and took a determined step, half inclined to follow him, until she remembered the strange cry she had heard in the snow, and went instead to the front door and pulled it open.

Anna, returning with an armful of swedes, found her on the doorstep, listening.

"Oh, do come in, for goodness' sake. You're getting covered in snow," she exclaimed.

"All right, all right. I only want to see if I can hear that noise again. And you needn't be so fierce."

"I'm sorry, but somebody's got to look after things. And what's the use of trying to keep the place warm if you leave the door wide open?"

Verity shuffled inside with a sigh and followed her into the kitchen.

The caldron was really boiling now and Anna hurriedly cut up a couple of swedes and dropped them into the bubbling water. Before long, the pungent smell of the boiling vegetables began to fill the room.

Brian returned and went across to his suitcase in the corner. But he still refused to be drawn out about his secret plan, no matter how Verity wheedled.

"No point talking at this stage—it mightn't come off," was all he would say, as he picked up his case and returned to the door.

"Oh, Brian, you're not going up to that freezing room again?" said Anna.

"It's not as cold as you'd think. I've been sitting up close to the chimney. And, anyway, I suppose the thatch helps to keep it warm," he replied. "Besides, I've got another jersey here in my case if I want it, and more socks."

"Looks as though you're moving house," mumbled Verity, eyeing his suitcase disapprovingly. "Aren't you happy down here with us or something?"

But all she got by way of reply was a long, slow wink from Brian as he left the room.

"Do you want to be called when tea is ready, or aren't you interested?" she shouted after him as a parting shot.

There was no reply, and a moment later they heard the creak of his footsteps overhead.

"Anyway, I'll lay the table," she decided, setting out the mugs and slates along the bench.

"And now," she went on, "shall I get in more sticks and break them up?"

"I wish you would," said Anna. "This old range uses up a terrific lot of wood and coal."

"It's fun, though, isn't it, looking after our cozy home," said Verity contentedly.

She carried in several loads of branches, then began to break them up, stacking them neatly along the wall beside the range.

Presently Brian's anxious face appeared around the door. "Not missing tea, am I? There's a good smell coming upstairs."

Verity lifted her head and sniffed. "So there is!" she exclaimed, jumping up in a scatter of sticks. "However have you managed to make swedes smell so good, Anna?" And she hurried across to the fireplace, eyeing the caldron with interest.

Anna laughed. "I can't pretend it's anything new, exactly," she said. "But there was so little bacon left that I put the last piece in with the swedes. So this time we'll have hot bacon for a change. And," she added impressively, "we'll have two courses, starting with swede and bacon soup!"

"Is it ready now? I'm absolutely starving," cried Verity, hopping impatiently from foot to foot.

Anna prodded the contents of the caldron with her cooking stick. "I think so. It feels softish now," she said. "Mugs first, for the soup."

She tilted the caldron on its crane, filling the mugs and handing them around. Brian sat for a moment, cradling his mug in his hands to warm them.

"I bet it was cold up there in the bedroom," said Verity, hoping to surprise him into giving some hint as to what he had been doing. But he merely nodded absently, then lifted his mug and gave his whole attention to the enjoyment of its contents.

"It's absolutely scrumptious, Anna," said Verity. "I've even got a bit of bacon in my soup." And she tipped back her head to allow the final drops to trickle into her mouth.

"I think it will be best to use our mugs for the next course too, instead of slates," decided Anna, fishing around the caldron with her stick to scoop up the pieces of bacon.

"Good idea," said Verity. "Then we can pretend it's stew for a change. I do wish, though, that our meals weren't always over so quickly here. Meals usually take too long in other places, but here they're always over much too soon."

Brian ate in a dream, and had no sooner finished than he slipped away upstairs. Whatever he was doing up there was clearly occupying all his thoughts.

"He seems to have forgotten all about helping with the jobs down here, now he's so busy with his old secret," complained Verity, as she and Anna went through the cowhouse to fetch a final load of wood and coal, in preparation for the long night.

"I wonder if it's still snowing," said Anna. She opened the front door a crack and a flurry of snow blew in around her.

"Oh dear, it's worse than ever," she exclaimed. "Our path to the well is getting covered up already."

Verity poked her head out too, oblivious of the whirling snow as she strained her ears to listen. "I still can't hear it," she remarked, as Anna pulled her inside and shut the door.

When they got back to the kitchen, Anna picked up their three mugs and hung them from a row of hooks along the shelf. "There, that makes it look more homey," she said, smiling. "And I'll put the dish of swedes up here as well, so they'll be properly iced for your midnight feast!"

"And I'll eat them too, you'll see!" cried Verity with a delighted laugh.

"And you know something," she went on more seriously. "You are just as good a looker-afterer as Susan— better in some ways. Yes, really, I mean it," she insisted, as Anna opened her mouth to interrupt. "You see, you think of ways to make it fun, as well as looking after things. That's what makes it such a good adventure."

"Oh, what a nice thing to say!" cried Anna, catching her sister in a quick, warm hug. "You've helped too, you know, by enjoying it all so much, and even liking my funny bits of cooking. That helps more than you know."

9

ANNA spent a restless night. She couldn't resist going to the door from time to time to see what was happening outside, but every time she went she wished she hadn't. The firelight from the kitchen did not reach as far as the front door, but there was just light enough to see that it was still snowing. And what she could not see she could feel, as the fine flakes settled on her hair and outstretched hands.

On one of these trips she realized with a shock of surprise that the screaming wind had stopped at last. But the silence was almost worse than the wind had been, making it seem as though they were the only living creatures left in a snowbound world. It was a comfort to return to the kitchen, with its cheerful fire and the quiet breathing of the other two as they slept.

By morning the snow had stopped again. Verity

opened the front door and peered out into the early light.

"It's deeper than ever," she reported. "Not up over the door like yesterday, but the path we dug to the well has disappeared, and the tree by the gate looks like a monstrous snowball now."

"We'll have to clear the path again. We'll need water," said Brian, coming to join her in the doorway.

"Have breakfast first to warm you. It won't be long," called Anna from the kitchen. She fetched the cold boiled swedes from the shelf, but the thought of eating them for breakfast was not inviting. So, after filling the three mugs with hot water, she returned the soggy swedes to the caldron.

"Come along now, and drink this while it's hot," she called. "And when you've emptied your mugs there'll be swede porridge to follow."

"How will we eat it without any spoons?" asked Verity.

"We'll have to make do with bits of wood. After all, lots of people eat with chopsticks," said Anna.

Verity laughed, but as she tackled the warm swedes, she wondered how she could ever have found real porridge dull. The mere thought of oatmeal swimming in creamy milk made it hard to swallow the yellow pulp in her mug, hungry though she was. They were all glad to push their empty mugs aside and prepare for the morning's work.

As they dug down into the soft new snow, their spades struck the ice that had formed over yesterday's path.

"Careful, it'll be dreadfully slippery. Remember Aunt Marian," warned Anna.

The well was easy to clear. They found they could brush off most of the snow with their hands. As soon as it was uncovered, they fetched the empty tins and jars and started to refill them. It was hard work, made harder by the difficulty of keeping their footing on the icy path.

"Just ordinary living is hard work in a place like this, isn't it?" said Verity. "There isn't any time for playing when you're having a real adventure."

Anna nodded. Yet she secretly thought it was becoming altogether too much of an adventure, and she was beginning to wonder when it would ever end. Brian worked in preoccupied silence—no way of guessing what he might be thinking about it all. She was thankful that Verity, at any rate, was thoroughly enjoying it, and she watched her now as she paused in her work to stare about in rapture.

"Oh, Anna, look!" she shouted suddenly. "The sun's coming out!"

They all stopped work to stand entranced as the world about them was transformed into a glittering fairyland, the sparkling light shimmering over the snow.

"It's like a Christmas card," said Verity. "Only much, much more beautiful. Oh, and that reminds me—it will be January 6 tomorrow, and I did so want to give Brian a wonderful Christmas."

"Well, aren't I having it?" he laughed, looking around on the snowy scene.

"I know, but I wanted you to have a Christmas tree and candles as well as snow," she said in a disappointed tone, bending again to her digging.

The sunshine put fresh energy into them all, and the work of clearing was going ahead at a great pace when Verity's head came up suddenly.

"Listen!" she cried. "There's my noise again. And it's not the wind, because there isn't any."

This time they all heard something, although it would have been hard to describe the feeble sound, and harder still to be sure where it was coming from.

"Whatever it is, it sounds like something in trouble. We'll simply have to try and find it," said Anna.

"It's going to take a lot more digging, whichever direction we go," said Brian, straightening up to look around the snow-filled yard.

"I'm positive it's over there where the snow is all piled up against the barn," insisted Verity. "That's where I thought it came from yesterday."

"There was a gate over there, I remember, leading into the farmyard, and a bit of wall joining it to the barn," said Anna, starting at once to dig.

They worked steadily until Brian's shovel struck something hard.

"The gate, I bet," he muttered, plunging his arm into the drift ahead. "Yes, here it is. I can feel the bars."

"And here's the wall," announced Anna, loosening the snow around the gatepost.

They were soon able to shake the worst of the snow from the gate and climb over it. Verity took a flying leap from the top bar and landed up to her chest in a snow-drift.

"Whew! It's like jumping into the swimming pool, only colder," she gasped, wiping the snow from her chin.

"Better work our way along the wall towards the barn," advised Anna. "I should imagine anything trying to find shelter would have made for the angle between the wall and the barn, when the snow first began."

"You mean whatever it is that's crying has been here ever since the snow began—but that's two days ago!" cried Verity, her eyes wide with horror.

"Nothing could have gotten here since," Anna pointed out.

Verity looked up to where the snow had been swept up against the side of the barn like some gigantic wave. It was hard to believe that anything could possibly be alive under all that snow. But even as she wondered, the little sound was repeated very faintly.

"It's over there all right, whatever it is," cried Brian, plunging his spade into the snow with renewed energy. Verity worked beside him, but as they neared the barn she dropped her shovel, finding it easier to work with her hands, pushing down up to her elbows and tossing the snow back between her legs as she dug.

"I think it might be wise if we all did that now," suggested Anna. "In case our sharp spades might hurt whatever is there."

"It's quicker this way, anyhow," panted Verity. "Oh, bother this old snow!" And she shook her head impatiently as a handful of snow slid from the roof of the barn, splashing her cheek as it fell.

"I don't like that at all. There might be more to come down," muttered Anna, glancing up apprehensively.

"Steady now, there's something here!" called Brian, suddenly stumbling to his knees as the snow crumbled beneath his groping hands.

The two girls plunged across to where he knelt and, crouching down beside him, found themselves looking into what appeared to be a sort of cavern, roofed with crusted snow.

"Something . . . moved . . . in there!" whispered Verity, reaching for Anna's hand. As she spoke, a long pale face appeared in the opening.

"A sheep—oh, the poor thing, buried under all this snow!" cried Anna pitifully, holding out her hands as the numbed creature lurched toward them. But after a couple of hobbling steps its legs folded under it, and it collapsed at their feet, making no attempt to rise.

"Is it going to die?" quavered Verity tremulously.

Before Anna had time to reply, Brian shouted again.

"There's another one here—oh, gosh, there seem to be a whole lot of them, all crowded together against the barn. Come on, both of you, dig for all you're worth."

Showers of snow flew out behind the three as they clawed at the close-packed snow, uncovering one dazed animal after another.

"This one's got bits of fluff sticking out of its mouth," exclaimed Verity, stopping her work to stare.

"Oh dear, that shows how starving it must be, poor thing," cried Anna. "Uncle Fred says snowed-up sheep sometimes try to eat each other's wool when they're really desperate with hunger."

"Eat wool! How absolutely ghastly!" cried Verity. "Shall I dig down and see if I can find some grass for it under the snow?"

"No, no, there isn't time. We must get the rest out quickly, before it snows again, or . . ." Anna left the sentence unfinished as she looked again toward the roof of the high barn, wondering anxiously whether the accumulated snow might suddenly slither down on top of them all like an avalanche.

"There are some at the back here, lying down," reported Brian as he burrowed deeper into the drift.

"Dead?" breathed Verity, afraid to look and yet unable to move away.

"Can't tell," he muttered. "Here, come and help me clear this corner, will you?"

It was Verity who uncovered the lamb, lying huddled

against the wall, with its mother standing over it.

"Oh, the little thing—it's quite newborn," she gasped, dropping on her knees beside it.

"A newborn lamb out here in all this snow?" cried Anna. "You mean, it's still alive?"

"Oh yes. I think he's even trying to bleat, only no sound comes out when he opens his mouth. Ah, but he's shivering. Come here, little one," she crooned, gathering the tiny creature into her arms and trying to pull her anorak around its quivering body.

"You'd better take it in by the fire at once, before it dies of cold," advised Anna. She stepped back to make room for Verity to pass, and as she did so, the lamb's bedraggled mother stumbled after her.

"Shall I take the mother too?" asked Verity.

"Looks as though she's coming anyhow," said Anna, as the anxious ewe picked her way over the scattered snow and trotted after Verity with a piteous little cry.

This tremulous sound had an immediate effect on the rest of the flock, and one numbed animal after another struggled to its feet and followed. By the time Verity turned in through the gate, the whole flock was behind her, surging toward the house.

"Can they all come indoors?" she called, pausing on the doorstep with the lamb in her arms. "Oh, never mind, they seem to be coming, whatever we say." And she disappeared into the house as the sheep jostled in through the door, pushing her in ahead of them.

Anna and Brian lingered behind for a final poke around in the tumbled snow, making sure there were no more animals buried.

"Amazing they weren't all frozen to death, buried under all this for two days and nights," marveled Anna with a sudden shudder. "I suppose being crammed together helped to keep them alive. Is that the lot?"

"Seems to be. I can't see any more," he said, backing out of the crumbling drift.

"Poor things," said Anna softly. "They must have come down from the mountain fields when the snow began, and huddled up against the barn for shelter. But with the wind blowing the snow the way it did, it must have just piled up all night and buried them. But let's go in now and see how the lamb is doing."

10

SOME of the bolder sheep had followed Verity into the kitchen, but the rest remained in a huddled group just inside the front door, too dazed to move aside as Anna and Brian pushed through them. A few were lying down again, their heads drooping dejectedly.

"They must be weak with hunger," said Anna, remembering the wool in the sheep's mouth.

"Do come in here and see the lamb. He's beginning to feed," called Verity, who was kneeling on the kitchen floor, watching the little creature delightedly.

"He's all right—he's got his mother," said Anna thankfully. "But how in the world are we going to feed the rest of them?"

She was surprised by a sudden laugh from Brian as he came into the room behind her.

"Well, those two have decided for themselves—they're eating my bed!" he chuckled, pointing to the corner, where a couple of sheep were tossing his carefully piled hay in all directions.

"Well, there's plenty more hay in the barn—that's one good thing," said Anna, with a sigh of relief. "And, of course, there are all those swedes!" she went on eagerly. "I remember seeing Uncle Fred put out swedes in the fields for the sheep when there wasn't enough grass for them one winter."

They spent the next half hour carrying swedes and armfuls of hay into the cowhouse, where the sheep were quick to follow.

"They'll need water too," decided Anna. "I'll take this bucket through for them."

The cowhouse was soon filled with the sound of steady munching.

"They make swedes sound so delicious," murmured Verity enviously.

"Which reminds me, I'd forgotten all about us," confessed Anna. "I must put our own swedes on to cook, or we won't have any dinner."

"Let me just try a little bit raw, in case it tastes as nice as it sounds," begged Verity. But it was no good. She couldn't pretend she really liked it, raw or cooked.

"Perhaps someone will come and rescue us soon," she said, feeling for the first time that even the nicest adventures might go on a bit too long.

"Why should anyone come, when nobody knows we're lost?" said Anna. "Mummy isn't expecting us home till the day after tomorrow, remember. She doesn't even know about Aunt Marian's accident yet."

"Uncle Fred might have written to tell her about it."

"Not Uncle Fred! Have you ever known him to write a letter? No point, anyway, when he thinks we are at home telling Mummy the news ourselves."

She broke off as a sudden thud sounded overhead. "That must be Brian up there again. What on earth can he find to do up there in this awful cold?"

"He says he's got a plan, but he won't tell what it is," said Verity resentfully. "I'm beginning to think he's rather a dull person, after all."

"Oh no, he's much too clever to be dull. I expect it's just that he doesn't like talking about his ideas until he's sure they are going to work out. But, as it happens, I've been trying to work out a plan myself."

"Oh, tell me!" pleaded Verity.

"Well, I'm wondering if it would be possible to make a pair of snowshoes, so that one of us could walk down to the road to get help."

"Oh, Anna, what a super idea. How will you make them?"

"That's what will need working out. But now I must go and get some wood for the fire, and perhaps you'll bring in a couple more swedes for ourselves."

"The sheep look better already," commented Verity,

as they made their way through the cowhouse. "You know, I'm really quite glad they've moved out here from the kitchen. They do smell rather, don't they, especially when they're wet."

"Perhaps they don't like our smell any better than we like theirs!" suggested Anna, smiling.

Verity went through to the barn and picked out the two nicest swedes she could find. Then, tempted by the sunshine, she decided to return across the yard and in through the front door.

The old house stood up dark and somber, its gray stone contrasting sharply with the dazzling snow piled high on every ledge and windowsill. A fringe of shining icicles hung under the roof, glittering in the sunlight, and small pockets of ice had formed here and there on the stonework. Suddenly she noticed lettering cut into a square stone slab built into the wall of the house directly above the door. Stepping closer, she spelled out PEN MYNYDD 1672.

For a moment, she couldn't remember where she had heard the name before. Then in a flash it came back to her, and she burst into the kitchen with the news.

"I say, you remember Pen Mynydd? Well, this is it."

Anna looked at her, puzzled.

"You know, Uncle Fred said he'd brought the sheep down as far as Pen Mynydd? Well, I've just seen the name and a date, cut into a stone over the front door."

"Ah," said Anna, beginning to understand. "Then

Uncle Fred must be the one who took over this land when the last people left the place. I suppose he's using it for grazing for his sheep and maybe for crops as well. So those must be his swedes in the barn."

"Whose swedes?" asked Brian, coming into the room and going across to hold his stiff hands to the fire.

"Uncle Fred's. Verity has just discovered that this farm is Pen Mynydd, the one he was talking about the other morning."

To their astonishment, Brian swung around from the fire, his whole face alight.

"Pen Mynydd!" he shouted. "Now we know where we are—that's all I need!"

"What on earth?" demanded Verity. "Whatever is the use of knowing our address? You surely don't expect someone to write you a letter and send it here?"

"No postman could deliver it if anyone did," said Anna laughing.

"Then what?" persisted Verity, eyeing her cousin curiously as he stood absently warming one hand at the fire, quite unruffled by their amused smiles.

"Well, I guess it's worth telling you my plan now, since there seems real hope of its working out," he said. "You see, I've been trying to think of a way of sending out an S.O.S. so somebody can come and rescue us."

"An S.O.S.!" Verity's cheeks were pink with sudden excitement. "How will you send it?"

"I've decided to send out my model plane with a message. Now that that awful wind has died down, it ought to be able to fly a mile or so, and I feel if I send it in the direction of the hospital and the main road, there is at least a chance that somebody might see it and pick it up. I only wish it was one of the kind with a diesel engine. People would be much more likely to notice a noisy thing like that. This one hardly makes a sound. However, it seems our only chance."

"Is your string as long as a mile?" asked Verity.

"Oh, I wouldn't use a control line. It must fly free," he explained.

"Then how will you get it back?"

"I probably never will," he answered quietly.

She caught her breath in a little gasp but, glancing at his face, decided to say nothing more.

It was Anna who asked, "What sort of message shall you send?"

Brian brightened as he replied: "That's why I wanted to know where we are, you see. The whole point of sending out a call for help is to tell people exactly where we are. So now that Verity has discovered the name of this house, I can do just that. However, the first thing is to finish assembling the plane. It's almost done."

"So that's what you've been doing upstairs!" cried Verity triumphantly.

"But whyever didn't you do it down here?" asked Anna. "It isn't as though much cooking goes on in this kitchen, and you would at least have been warm."

"Easier where I can spread it out all over the floor, with no danger of getting it stepped on," he replied.

"Who did you think would step on it?" asked Verity suspiciously. But when he left the room without replying, she turned to Anna. "You're right," she said. "He isn't dull. I know *I* couldn't bear to lose my lovely new plane which I'd only just made, could you?" Without waiting for Anna's reply, she went on: "And you know something else? The sheep will be rescued too."

"I know, I'd realized that," said Anna.

"He's coming down. What now, I wonder?" said Verity, as footsteps came clattering down the stone stairs.

"Either of you got a bit of thread?" asked Brian, appearing in the doorway.

"Afraid not," admitted Anna. "Susan is the only one who ever has sewing things."

"I've got to find something to test the balance of the plane," he explained, looking helplessly around the kitchen. "If only there were curtains or something here, then I might be able to pull out a thread."

"I know the very thing!" cried Verity, darting toward her suitcase. "When I was at Aunt Marian's, I noticed a string where the shoulder of my pajamas is beginning to come unstitched. I bet we could unravel it a bit more—all right, Anna, I know what you're going to say, but I'm positive Mummy won't mind if it means us being rescued." And opening the case, she pulled out her blue pajama top.

"There, how's that?" she asked, showing Brian the loop of unraveled thread. "Does it matter being rather crinkly?"

"Not a bit, the weight of the plane will soon straighten that out. Steady on, though. No need to go so fast, or you'll break the thread before we've got enough."

But the thread unraveled easily, and he soon had the length he needed.

He was making for the stairs when Anna called him back. "Better have dinner first," she said. "It's dull, I'm afraid, but at least it's something hot."

For once, even Verity was glad when the meal was over and Brian disappeared upstairs again. There was a long silence, but at last he reappeared, carrying the finished plane with the blue thread attached to its upper wing.

"Oh, how beautiful it is," murmured Verity, putting out a gentle finger to touch the graceful little model.

"I'm only sorry I've nothing to color it with," he said regretfully. "It would be so much more conspicuous against the snow if it were red or orange or even black."

"Is it ready to fly now?" asked Verity eagerly.

"Not quite. I haven't got it perfectly balanced yet. That's why I needed the thread. The balance must be absolutely right, or it won't fly properly."

He made a loop in the end of the thread and slipped it over a cup hook on the shelf, allowing the plane to hang free.

"You can see it's a bit lopsided still," he pointed out, stepping back to study it critically.

"How can you get it right?" asked Anna.

"I'll probably have to fix a bit of weight just here, in the rear of the nose-weight recess," he explained, looking around for something he might use. He picked up a piece of firewood and broke off a tiny piece and inserted it into the recess.

"Too bulky," he decided. "I really need something heavier." He wandered off into the cowhouse and they heard a pattering rustle as the sheep moved out of his way.

"They're much more timid now that they're fed," observed Anna. "It was only hunger that made the poor things so unnaturally tame when they first came in here."

When Brian returned, he had a collection of bits and pieces in his hand: a twist of wire, half a rusted nail, a scrap of tin, and other oddments. He inserted one after another into the plane, standing back and squinting his eyes to study the effect of each.

Anna grinned privately to herself, guessing what an effort it must be for the restless Verity to stand patiently watching this slow process. But at long last Brian was satisfied and his face relaxed in a slow wide smile.

"O.K. All ready now for flying trials," he announced.

11

*F*LYING trials?'' Verity was dismayed. "Do you mean the plane isn't ready to go off with the message even now?''

"Good gracious, no. We can't let her set off on her one important flight without making certain she can fly properly,'' explained Brian patiently.

Anna began to see why her stopped watch had not worried him. She had never before met anyone so unaware of the passing of time.

"Do you do the trials here in the house?'' asked Verity, fidgeting with impatience.

"No, we must find a suitable place outside,'' he replied.

"Where? In the yard?'' Verity was already half across the room, dragging on her anorak as she made for the door.

"No need for all that hurry," said Brian placidly. "Pointless, going out into the cold before we need. I may just as well do the winding up in here by the fire."

"Winding up? What do you have to wind?"

"This rubber band attached to the propeller. That's what makes it fly."

"How long will it take to wind?" she asked dejectedly, dropping her anorak on the floor.

"I'll have to make about two hundred turns for the trial run," he answered tranquilly.

"Two hundred turns! But that will take absolute ages."

Anna exploded into sudden laughter. "Oh, Verity, you'd better come and help me over here before you burst!" she said. "These sticks need breaking up. They're too long for the grate as they are."

Brian looked from one to the other, vaguely puzzled, then turned his attention to what he was doing, finding it a good deal easier to understand than his impatient cousins.

When the sticks were done, Verity tiptoed into the cowhouse to see the lamb.

"He's fast asleep, lying beside his mother," she reported on her return. "And the others are lying down quite peacefully, chewing the cud. Isn't our dear Pen Mynydd a kind old house, sheltering us all like this?"

Brian decided the best place for the launching was a flat spot behind the farm.

"We'll go higher up the hill for the big flight, to give her a good open range," he said. "But this will do for a start."

"Are you going to use a control line for the trial flight?" asked Anna.

"No need. She won't go all that far on this short rubber band. Once I see how she flies, I'll put in a longer band for the big flight."

Anna saw Verity shrug her shoulders at this prospect of still another delay, but Brian was too preoccupied to notice.

Raising the plane to shoulder level, he aimed it carefully. Then, holding the tail lightly in one hand, he released first the propeller and then the tail, and suddenly the little plane was airborne, skimming away from them over the dazzling snow.

Brian darted after it, plunging through the deep snow, his arms thrashing the air to help his floundering progress.

"He can move fast enough when he wants to," muttered Verity as she and Anna struggled after him.

"She's perfectly O.K.," he called, as he pounced on the plane and picked it up. "All the same, I'd better give her a couple more trials, just to make quite sure of her before I change to the longer band."

"But what about the light? It's beginning to get dark already," said Anna hesitantly.

"So it is," he said, glancing around in surprise. "Never mind, we'll send her out first thing tomorrow. Better in the morning, actually. More chance of being spotted."

"What if it's snowing again tomorrow?" muttered Verity.

"It just mustn't be, that's all!" he laughed.

Verity kicked out savagely at the snow as she fought down her disappointment. But Anna saw the sense of Brian's decision.

"He's right, you know," she mused. "The plane would be far more likely to be overlooked if we sent it off at this time of day. Nobody's likely to be out at dusk if he can help it in this weather. Besides, we haven't written the message yet."

"No, we haven't. What are we going to say?" asked Verity, brightening at once. "And where will you fix the message anyway?" she hurried on, giving no one time to answer her first question.

"I'll write it on the upper wing," said Brian. "Safer than a bit of paper, which might get blown away."

"Besides, the finder might never think of looking inside for a message," Anna pointed out.

"Where are you going now?" asked Verity, as Brian turned back toward the house.

"Going to do the winding up by the fire again. It's too jolly cold out here," he said, leading the way indoors.

While Brian wound up in preparation for the next trial flight, the two girls brought in wood and coal and water for still another night, discussing the wording of their S.O.S. as they worked.

"We must make it a really thrilling message, like the ones shipwrecked people put in bottles," said Verity, her mind busy with the tale she would have to tell at school next term.

But Brian insisted that the message must be simple.

"The less we say the better," he decided. "No one will bother to read a whole long rigmarole. I suggest something like 's.o.s. SNOWED UP IN PEN MYNYDD FARM NEAR HILLSIDE HOSPITAL,' and our three names underneath. The finder won't be expecting a message, so we've got to catch his attention straightaway."

He gave the little plane three more trial flights, making minute adjustments after each. Eventually he was satisfied.

"Fine," he said, retrieving the plane for the last time. "I'll put in the new rubber band now and write the message on the wing. Then she'll be all set to fly off tomorrow morning."

They watched him write the message in clear black capitals, going over each letter several times until it stood out boldly.

"Whoever picks it up can't help seeing that," said Anna.

"Especially the S.O.S." said Verity. "And SNOWED UP looks exciting, don't you think?"

12

*I*T isn't snowing, anyhow," reported Verity, peering out into the half light next morning.

"Then you and I had better do all the jobs ourselves, to leave Brian free to concentrate on Operation Rescue Flight," decided Anna.

"Operation Rescue Flight—what a thrilling name for it," cried Verity excitedly.

But she was not so excited when she discovered that this flight was going to take a good deal longer to prepare than the previous ones.

"He says he's got to wind this one eight hundred times —just imagine it, *eight hundred!*" she confided to Anna as they went to get the coal. "It's no use even trying to talk to him now, because he's only really thinking about his counting all the time. It makes him talk in jerks, like this: 'We must give the rescuers time . . . one hundred and forty-three, hundred and forty-four, hundred and forty-five . . . to get up here after finding the plane . . . one hundred and forty-eight, hundred and forty-nine . . .' "

"As bad as the countdown for a space flight," commented Anna. "Except that this is a count-up."

At last, after what seemed to Verity the longest morning of her whole life, the plane was ready to take off, and they all trooped up to the chosen launching spot on a little rise above the gate.

Even now, there was one last minute hold-up.

"I say, Anna, I think it might be an idea to add the date to our message, so the finder knows when the plane set out," said Brian. "Can you fish the pen out of my pocket and write it. I can't let go of the plane myself."

Anna found the pen and he held the plane steady for her to add the date.

"What is it, anyway?" she asked, pausing. "The sixth?"

"That's right." He nodded.

"January 6!" echoed Verity. "Old Christmas Day, when we were going to give you a real English Christmas."

"Well, I'm having a real Welsh Christmas, snow and all," he reminded her.

But there was no time now for further talk. The great moment had arrived.

Brian raised the plane, held it steady for a moment,

and then released it, and it shot into the air with an exciting whir of its small propeller. They held their breath as they watched it skim away, flying strongly over the snow toward the wooded slope up which they themselves had climbed three days ago.

Brian stood watching the little plane until it finally dipped beyond the trees and disappeared.

"Suppose somebody finds it straightaway. How long will it take them to get up here?" wondered Verity.

"Much longer than it took us to get up here on Monday," said Anna. "All this snow has turned it into a very different place, almost a different world. Anyhow, rescue or no rescue, we must eat. I'll go down and see to it."

"Our Christmas dinner! I wonder what we are going to have!" said Verity with a twinkle.

Anna grinned back at her. "It will be Pen Mynydd soup today, followed by swede Christmas pudding!" she said gaily, her spirits soaring at the thought of the little rescue plane speeding on its way.

However, she and Brian were well aware that this particular rescue bid might not come off. Everything depended on somebody happening to find their little plane in what they knew to be an unpopulated stretch of country.

"Once down on the ground, it will be a very small speck in a very big waste of snow," he said thoughtfully.

"And if nobody finds it?" questioned Verity.

"That's what we've got to think out," said Anna. "Even without the drifted snow, it would be an awful long way for us to walk down to the road."

During the short climb to launch the plane, she had realized the depth of the snow around them.

It was now that she suddenly remembered her idea of making snowshoes.

"Of course I know it would be awfully difficult to walk down, even wearing snowshoes," she said doubtfully. "But it might be an idea if nobody finds our plane."

So, as soon as the meal was over, she and Brian put their heads together in a serious discussion of how snowshoes might be made with the materials they had at hand. They decided to experiment with boards of wood tied to their boots with string.

Verity wandered away, mulling over a secret plan of her own. It was not an escape plan, but something she felt to be every bit as important. She had decided that she was going to give Brian a Christmas tree to make up for the loss of his plane.

But he had mentioned a Christmas tree and candles. The tree she could manage somehow, but what about the candles? She was crossing the passage toward the front door when suddenly she pulled up short and stood frowning, as she struggled to remember. Surely, surely she had seen a candle somewhere very recently? She had not thought about it until this moment, but now she

clearly remembered how it looked, at the back of a dark
shelf, with an empty jam jar and a dusty bit of old dry
soap. This was not the sort of muddle one would find in
Aunt Marian's well-ordered house, so she must have seen
it somewhere here in Pen Mynydd. She stood biting her
lips in perplexity as she sent her thoughts into every
empty room in turn.

Suddenly her face lit up and she darted across the passage into the little pantry through which she had made
her first entry into the house.

The snow-blocked window made it darker than she
remembered, but she stooped to the lower shelf, which
had been on a level with her eyes as she wriggled in
through the window. And there was the candle, rolled to
the back of the shelf, as she remembered.

She took it out and examined it. It was nearly new,
and she slipped it into her pocket with a little smile of
satisfaction.

Returning to the kitchen, she found the other two
crouched among an assortment of planks and slats of
wood scattered over the floor.

"The trouble is, they're going to be so heavy," Anna
was saying in a discouraged tone. "I'm afraid they will
only sink into the snow. I think real snowshoes must be
made of something lighter."

"Leather, probably, stretched on wicker frames,"
mused Brian.

They were far too absorbed to notice what Verity was

doing, as she moved across to the fireplace and, reaching up to the mantelpiece, found Brian's packet of matches. Slipping these into her pocket with the candle, she went through the far door. She made her way down the length of the cowhouse, walking slowly so as not to disturb the sheep, some peacefully chewing the cud, others pulling at the hay or nibbling swedes. The lamb lay fast asleep on a pile of hay below the end manger.

Pulling up the hood of her anorak, she went out through the half door at the far end, gasping a little as the icy cold caught her breath and stung her eyes to tears.

She stumbled through the deep snow, struggling across to the far side of the yard where she had noticed a fir tree growing against the wall. It was weighed down with snow, but she shook this off one of the lower branches, revealing dark pine needles hung with shining icicles.

"Just like Christmas decorations," she murmured happily.

Taking care not to loosen the icicles, she bent the branch until it snapped away from the trunk of the tree.

Brian had left a battered bucket in the barn, so full of holes that it could not even be used for holding coal. But, after stuffing the holes with hay, she was able to fill it with loose earth shaken from the piled swedes. She now stood her branch of icicles in the bucket, pressing the earth tightly around the stem until it stood firmly upright, making such an enchanting little Christmas tree that she laughed aloud with pleasure.

She carried it carefully into the cowhouse, where she lifted it onto the wide rim of the end manger, moving quietly so as not to wake the lamb still fast asleep below. The light was already beginning to fail, and she realized she must hurry before it got too dark to see what she was doing.

She remembered seeing her mother stand a candle on a saucer once, firmly stuck in a little pool of its own wax. She now found she could stand her own candle in the same way on a piece of slate.

"Almost as steady as a proper candlestick," she said with satisfaction as she set it up beside the little tree, experimenting until she found a spot where its light shone through the icicles, making them sparkle and shine.

There was something in the strange half-light that lent an unearthly quality to the little tree, with its spangles of muted light quivering against the deepening dusk. Verity stood transfixed for a moment, astonished by the delicate beauty she had created. Then she ran back to the kitchen and summoned the others.

As Anna came in through the cowhouse door, she caught her breath in a little gasp that was almost a sob.

"Why, Verity, it's like a sort of Christmas vision," she whispered, gazing from the shining tree on the manger to the new-born lamb asleep on the hay below.

"With the sheep all standing around like a Christmas crib," added Verity.

"And all seen by candlelight in a snowbound cattle shed. It just couldn't be more perfect," finished Anna softly.

Brian was silent for so long that Verity glanced at him uncertainly.

"You . . . you do like it, don't you?" she asked at last.

Even now he did not reply immediately, and when he did his voice seemed to come from far away.

"I know I'll see other trees in other years, maybe even some with candles," he said musingly, "but I know I shall never again in all my life see a Christmas tree as beautiful as this one. It is so small and simple and so right, standing here in the cattle shed on Old Christmas Day."

The candle flame swelled and wavered in a draft from the warped old window, and they stood watching it in silence as the brief twilight faded into darkness.

"Couldn't we sing some Christmas carols while the candle lasts?" suggested Verity. " 'Away in a manger' would be a good one to start with, don't you think?"

13

ONE carol led to another.

"How about 'While shepherds watched their flocks by night'?" said Verity. "Because we've got the flock by night, even if we haven't any shepherds."

Her eyes strayed toward the little window as they sang the familiar words, and suddenly she saw the wavering light of a lantern swinging over the snow. She broke off in the middle of a verse to run to the window.

"It looks like carol singers coming across the yard," she began. "Or . . . or . . . well, they really look more like shepherds—could they be?" she added in an awed whisper as footsteps sounded on the step outside. Then the heavy door swung open and a tall figure stamped into the passage.

"Uncle Fred! Oh, Uncle Fred, you've come!" cried

Anna, her voice breaking on a sudden sob of relief as she hurled herself into his arms.

"There now, nothing more for you to worry about. We'll have you safe back home in no time," he said, giving her shoulder a comforting pat. "But first of all we could do with a warm-up, couldn't we, boys? This bitter old wind is enough to freeze one solid. And I see you've managed to light yourselves a fire," he added, as with his arm still around her shoulders he went through to the firelit kitchen, closely followed by his two companions.

"My, but you've made yourselves mighty snug in here!" he exclaimed admiringly. "It looks real homey, almost as good as when the old Taylors lived up here a few years back."

The three men gathered silently around the fire, gratefully holding their numbed hands to the blaze, while the melting snow slid off their steaming clothes to collect in little pools around their feet.

It was Brian who broke the silence. He had been standing in the doorway, watching the men intently, and now, unable to bear the suspense any longer, he burst out, "My plane—did you find my plane with the S.O.S.?"

"Indeed we did," said Uncle Fred, turning around with a broad smile. "Jim and Stan here found it on the road below." Then, more soberly, he added, "And but for that little plane we'd never have known you were here at all."

"I suppose you thought we were safe at home?" said Anna in a small voice.

"Ah, we did that," he said. "Poor old Sue was in a fine taking, I can tell you, when the snow came on so heavy after I got back Monday dinnertime. I told her you'd left the coach stop, but then she was fussed in case the coach might get stuck in a snowdrift somewhere! Anyway, nothing would satisfy her but to go struggling down to the kiosk Monday afternoon and phone the coach station. And of course they told her the eleven o'clock coach got through all right. So we naturally reckoned you were safe home ahead of the worst of the storm."

"Poor Sue," said Anna understandingly.

"Whatever did she say when she heard about our S.O.S.?" Verity asked, wide-eyed.

"What indeed!" chuckled Uncle Fred with a rueful smile. "Well, of course she wanted to come up here with us now herself. But I reckoned we'd have enough to do getting three of you down without having a fourth on our hands. So I persuaded her to build up a roaring fire for you at home and get a hot meal ready—but bless me, I almost forgot—" And he broke off to reach for a haver-sack that he had dropped on the floor as he came in. "She's sent up a hot drink for you here in a thermos, and I don't know what-all besides."

"I was wondering what you had in there," said Verity, edging closer to watch him undo the buckles. "Ooh I say, it's a real banquet!" she cried joyfully as he pulled out bulging packets of cake and biscuits.

For a while the only sounds in the kitchen were the

drip-drip-drip of the men's wet clothes and the rustle of paper bags as the three children fell hungrily on their banquet.

When every last crumb was eaten, Verity wiped her fingers on her slacks and turned to her uncle. "Mind you," she said loyally, "we've had good food up here too. Anna's really super at cooking swedes."

"Oh Verity," interrupted Anna with a grin. But Verity shook her head emphatically. "No, really, it's absolutely true, isn't it, Brian?"

But Brian was already caught up in another conversation as Jim and Stan plied him with questions about his plane, wanting to know all the details of its construction and flying trials and the eventual launching in the snow.

And Anna wanted questions answered, too. "This snow," she asked, turning to her uncle, "is it bad at home as well as here in Wales?"

He threw up his hands. "Never known anything like it for years and years," he said. "It's all over the country —telephone wires down, trains delayed, no post, no newspapers, nothing. I couldn't even get down to visit your aunt again after I left her Monday."

"And to think of you kids up here through it all," marveled Jim.

"You know, I thought you were carol singers when I saw you coming in with the lantern," said Verity, grinning up at him.

"Well, to tell the truth, you sounded more like angels,"

he said, smiling. "Although it beats me how you could feel like singing after three days in this dump."

"Ah, but it isn't a dump, not really," she said. "We've had a box bed to sleep in and a gorgeous fire day and night. So it's really been a marvelous adventure, with Anna to cook our meals and make this place into a cozy home, and Brian to send out an S.O.S. when it was time to be rescued."

"And you to make it into a Christmas I shall remember all my life," Brian reminded her.

They were startled by a sudden exclamation from Uncle Fred, who had moved across to the far door to investigate a movement that caught his eye in the candle-lit cowhouse.

"Sheep!" he shouted in astonishment. "And *my* sheep, if I'm not mistaken," he went on, bending to examine the earmark of the nearest animal. "Well, I thought I'd lost this lot for sure, buried somewhere out there in a snowdrift. I've been out with the dogs in the fields above, searching for them these last three days."

"You were right about the snowdrift," Anna told him. "They were buried all right, poor things. Verity heard them first, and we dug them out yesterday and brought them in here in the warm. We've been feeding them on hay and swedes."

"And look!" interrupted Verity. "There's even a lamb, born out there under all that mass of snow!" And she picked up the little creature to show him.

"Well, this one would have died for certain," Uncle Fred remarked thoughtfully. "And most probably the others too, by this time. I reckon you kids have saved the whole flock between you. And without so much as a dog to help you, either. Beats all, that does."

He stood staring around at the animals as though even now he could scarcely believe they were real.

"And what's more," he decided presently, "I think I may as well leave them up here for the night, seeing as they're well supplied with food and shelter. Then I'll come up with the dogs in the morning and fetch them down in daylight. Which reminds me, I suppose the rest of us had better be making tracks for home to put poor Susan's mind at rest."

"I'll fetch our cases," said Anna, hurrying back to the kitchen.

"And we'd best damp down that fire a bit," remarked her uncle as he followed her through the door.

"Don't let's us two go before we've absolutely got to," whispered Verity, edging close to Brian.

"You bet I'm not wasting one second of this if I can help it," he replied, fixing his eyes on the little tree which still shone bravely from the manger. Its icicles were beginning to melt, and they stood in silence, watching the glittering drops sparkle in the candlelight as they fell.

"All the same, I'm afraid our lovely Christmas is almost over," he said with a sigh.

"I know," she said regretfully, "but we really will remember it all our lives, like you said, won't we?"

As the long shed grew darker, the sheep's eyes caught the candlelight, gleaming softly green in the darkness.

"Like lots of little pale green lamps," said Verity.

"Or a stable full of stars," said Brian.

As he spoke, the candle quietly guttered out, bringing their little Christmas to an end.